OMM

SON

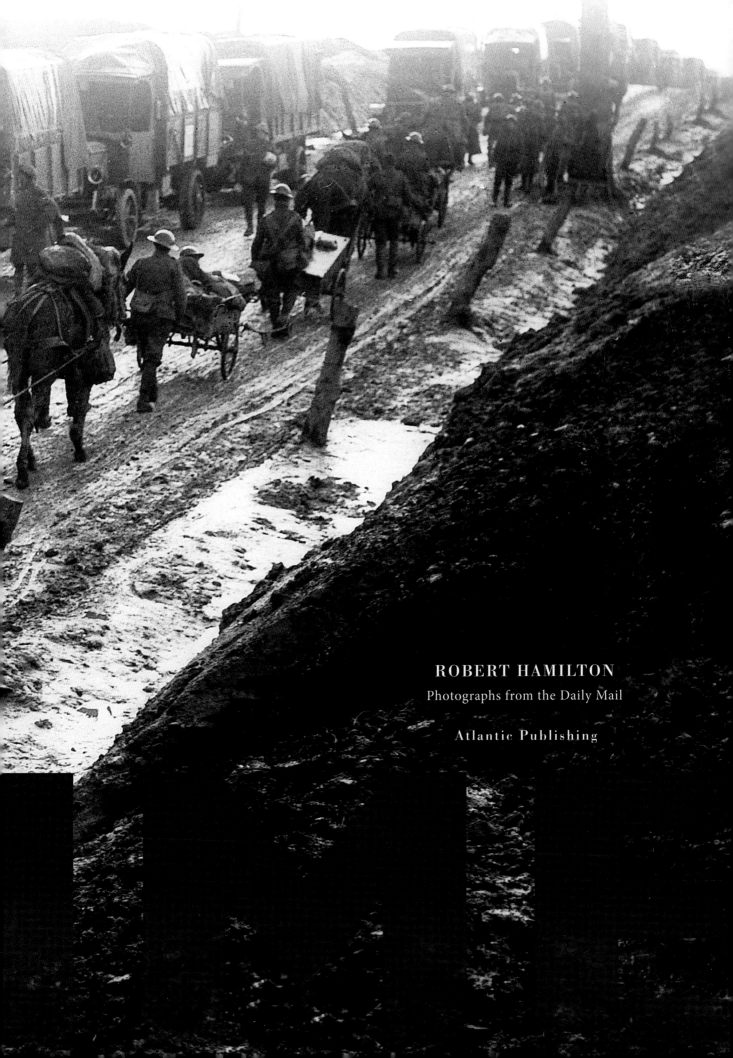

ROBERT HAMILTON

Photographs from the Daily Mail

Atlantic Publishing

BATTLES OF THE SOMME, 1916

First phase: July 1916

First day on the Somme, 1 July

Battle of Albert, 1–13 July

Battle of Bazentin Ridge, 14–17 July

Battle of Fromelles, 19 – 20 July

Second phase: July – September 1916

Battle of Delville Wood, 15 July – 3 September

Battle of Pozières, 23 July – 3 September

Battle of Guillemont, 3 – 6 September

Battle of Ginchy, 9 September

Third phase: September–November 1916

Battle of Flers–Courcelette, 15 – 22 September

Battle of Morval, 25 – 28 September

Battle of Thiepval, 26 – 28 September

Battle of Transloy Ridge, 1 October – 18 October

Battle of the Ancre Heights, 1 October – 11 November

Battle of the Ancre, 13 – 18 November

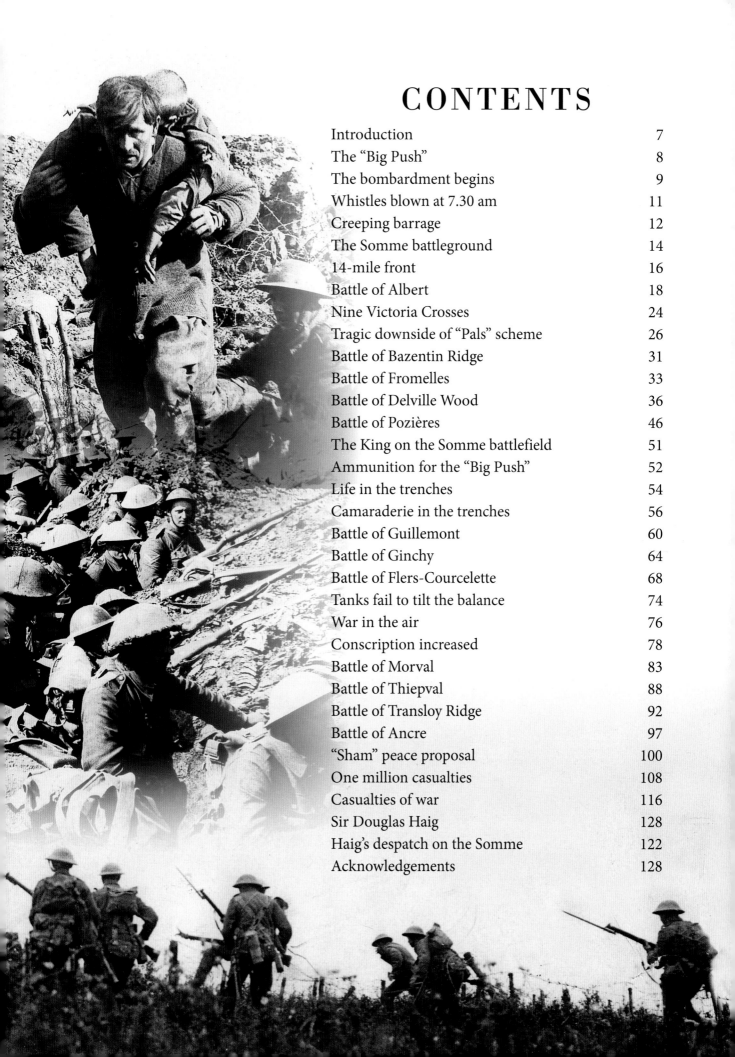

CONTENTS

INTRODUCTION

Of all the theatres in which the 1914-18 conflict was fought, it is the trench warfare on the Western Front that springs most readily to mind. And of all the bloody, attritional engagements that took place along that snaking, 400-mile front during three-and-a-half years of static warfare, the Battle of the Somme stands apart. A single syllable summons to mind not geography but history; not the verdant Picardy countryside or the river that meanders through it but cloying mud, flying bullets and scenes of unspeakable carnage that played out in the summer and autumn of 1916.

The plan was simple enough: to stretch Germany's resources to breaking point with concerted Allied attacks across all fronts. In the west, a joint British-French advance astride the Somme river would punch a hole in the enemy line. By the time battle was joined at the end of a week-long shell storm on 1 July 1916, Sir Douglas Haig's British Expeditionary Force had assumed the senior role in the operation. French troops had been pouring into Verdun since February, when that historic fortress town came under sustained German onslaught. The Somme offensive thus also served as a welcome relieving attack for the beleaguered French. It succeeded, at least, in that regard.

Bald statistics mark it out. 57,000 BEF casualties on Day One alone, one-third of those dead. Over a million killed or wounded by the time the opposing generals counted the cost five months later. A few miles of ground changed hands. A century on, the "Big Push" of 1916 continues to divide opinion. For some it was a well-intentioned attempt to force an end to the stalemate and laid the platform for the successes that were to follow. For others it remains an ill-conceived byword for futile, industrial-scale bloodletting. The opposing views are as deeply entrenched as the combatants themselves before the order to go over the top was given in a shrill blast of the whistle.

This is the story of the Battle of the Somme; not the hoped-for decisive engagement of the Great War but for many its defining episode; a desperate 20-week struggle that has become synonymous with heroism and sacrifice, with the hellish horrors of trench warfare.

The "Big Push"

In November 1916 the Allies' major offensive of the year wound down. A *Times* correspondent said of the five-month Somme campaign that it had been "not one battle but 50 battles, and 50 victories". That 100 per cent approval rating, understandable when a white-hot war was being waged and managing the national mood was a serious business, plummeted when the grim facts became public knowledge. The Somme became synonymous with industrial-scale blood-letting, wastefulness of human life for marginal gain. It also put under the microscope the reputations of those who formulated the plan and cleaved to it with unbending faith even as the death toll soared.

Ending the stalemate

The Allies went into 1916 intent on stretching Germany's resources to breaking point. Russia and Italy would play their part in a co-ordinated attack, while the focal point of the Western Front offensive would be an Anglo-French assault on a 25-mile stretch of the enemy line astride the River Somme. For Sir Douglas Haig, who replaced Sir John French as BEF commander in December 1915, the "Big Push" offered the chance to wrest the initiative, to end the stalemate and return to a war of movement. The shell shortage had been addressed, and "Kitchener's Army" was being readied. After an artillery bombardment the like of which had never been seen, those recruits would stroll through the enemy line unhindered. "You will meet nothing but dead and wounded Germans," said General Sir Henry Rawlinson, commander of the newly-formed Fourth Army and the man charged with implementing the plan. His confident prediction didn't stop him from having ambulance trains ready to take heavy casualties.

Haig's timing

The fact that Verdun was under siege from late February made little difference to the Allied operation, except with regard to the timing. By early summer the beleaguered French needed the Somme attack to begin sooner rather than later in order to relieve the pressure on their historic fortress town. For Haig there was a balance to be struck between coming to the aid of an alliance partner and not pressing the New Army into service too soon. Late June gave due weight to both considerations. When the attack was launched, France could commit only five divisions; Britain would be very much the senior partner.

"You will meet nothing but dead and wounded Germans."

Above: The calm before the storm. Two infantrymen share a quiet moment on the eve of the Somme offensive.

The bombardment begins

The week-long bombardment began on 24 June. Even as the first of over a million shells pounded the German line, the plan began to unravel. The infantry upon whose heads the bombardment rained incessantly went to ground. And in the chalky subsoil of the battlezone the Germans dug very deep, over 30 feet in places. While they were safely ensconced in their bunkers, shrapnel shells exploded harmlessly above. Many were duds. Crucially, only a fraction of the ordnance had the explosive power to penetrate to the depths where the subterranean army had taken refuge. Add in the fact that those million-and-a-half shells were spread over a vast area and the picture became even worse for Haig and Rawlinson. The former did not take criticism well; no one dared pass on the information that the bombardment had not had the desired effect. Thus on 30 June 1916, the eve of battle, Haig noted in his diary: "The wire has never been so well cut, nor the artillery preparation so thorough".

German infantry prepared

The guns at last fell silent on the morning of 1 July. With a final destructive flourish, huge mines that had been laid beneath the enemy line were exploded. The effect of these was chiefly the same as the other shells: churning up the same ground, launching the same barbed wire into the air until gravity delivered it back to earth. As it came to rest for the final time, the German infantry needed no clearer signal that the Allies were on the march. They emerged from the underground sanctuaries to set up their machine-gun emplacements in plenty of time to greet the advance.

No one dared pass on the information that the bombardment had not had the desired effect.

Below: Lancashire Fusiliers fix their bayonets prior to assault. By the start of the Somme offensive one million manganese steel helmets were delivered to the front line. Weighing two pounds each, they were designed to withstand shrapnel travelling at 750 feet per second.

The German infantry emerged from the underground sanctuaries to set up their machine-gun emplacements in plenty of time to greet the advance.

Above: **This new recruit, believed to be Private Joseph Bailey from the Sheffield Pals, became one of the first soldiers to be killed in the offensive. Eight battalions went "over the top" on the first day with the three Pals battalions suffering the heaviest casualty rate.**

JULY 3, 1916

The first day's gains

A great battle had been fought. Another is being fought, and many more have yet to be fought. It will probably be called in England the Battle of Montauban and in France the Battle of the Somme. But, whatever we call it, or however we judge it, we must think of it as a battle of many battles, not to be likened in duration or extent, or perhaps intention, to such affairs as Neuve Chapelle or Loos.

It is and for many days will continue to be siege warfare, in which a small territorial gain may be a great strategical gain; and the price we must pay is to be judged by another measure than miles or furlongs or booty.

We are laying siege not to a place but to the German army – that great engine which had at last mounted to its final perfection and utter lust of dominion.

In the first battle, which I saw open with incredible artillery fury at 6 o'clock this morning, we have beaten the Germans by greater dash in the infantry and vastly superior weight in munitions. I may, perhaps, claim to be in some position to estimate methods and results. I watched the night bombardments, both German and British. I saw at close quarters the hurricane of the morning bombardment, which heralded that first gay, impetuous, and irresistible leap from the trenches, many of which I had visited earlier, knowing what was to come.

Whistles blown at 7.30 am

In the British forward trenches whistles were blown at 7.30 am to signal the start of the attack. Some in the first wave that went over the top kicked footballs ahead of them, as if to blithely suggest that this would be the extent of their day's shooting. The men who struck out into no-man's-land were encumbered with kit weighing up to 70lb – heavy enough for a footslog over open ground; an enormous burden when the bullets began flying. Some wore reflective material on their backs to ensure that any supporting artillery fire went well over their heads. But it was the shellfire in front of them that did the damage. In their thousands soldiers of the new citizen army were cut to pieces, every fallen body exposing those behind to deadly fire. Where gaps in the barbed wire had been opened up, these attracted both oncoming soldiers and the attention of German machine-gunners. The laudable idea of encouraging men from the same community to join up together rebounded as some "Pals battalions" sustained heavy losses, leaving entire communities bereft. Still the troops ventured forth towards the enemy, at walking pace and in orderly lines as instructed. It was "as though they were going to the theatre", said one German soldier of the sedate advance.

Above left: A column of the East Yorkshire Regiment march into action along a peaceful country lane. Many of those fighting on the Somme were Kitchener's recruits and this was to be their first taste of the battlefield.

Left: For the first time the British commanders planned to use the tactic of the "creeping barrage"; a line of artillery fire moving forward just ahead of the advancing infantrymen.

Below: The Northumberland Fusiliers were one of the first regiments to go over the top at La Boiselle. The village was an important strategic target and successfully fell to the Allies on 6 July.

GOMMECOURT.

BRITISH FAILURE THAT WON THE DAY.

MARCH THROUGH A DEATH ZONE.

MAIN GERMAN FORCE PINNED DOWN.

MR. BEACH THOMAS IN FRICOURT.

Mr. Beach Thomas describes below first his visit to Fricourt and then the most glorious feat of the battle, the British attack at Gommecourt against the Germans' heaviest mass, an attack that failed at the spot but made possible success elsewhere.

From W. BEACH THOMAS.

PRESS CAMP, FRANCE,
Monday.

This morning, the third day of the battle, I was able to penetrate into Fricourt village itself and move up close to the edge of the wood some 500 yards behind our infantry, just at the time when they completed their brilliant attack across the base of the German wedge left at this place by the fighting of the first day.

Midland and Northern troops, attacking, the one from the north, the others from the south, joined hands just before noon at the base of the German wedge and put the finishing touch on a singularly well-executed manœuvre.

The regiments to the south, moving from the direction of the newly conquered village of Mametz, soon cleared the wood in front of them—just behind Fricourt Wood proper. The others were held up for a little while by a machine gun hidden in the edge of a copse. The fire of this gun could be heard rattling in little angry bouts whenever a group of men showed themselves; and apparently it could not be exactly located. But the check was a short one. The gun was outflanked, our troops made their way both across the open ground and down trenches into the scarified wood and were soon in touch with the other party. The German promontory was cut right across at the base and every man behind the cut was in our hands.

As I made my way well up into the village a north-country soldier

ing place, were quite indistinguishable. You could distinguish nothing. I mistook a revolving corn grinder for an engine of war and found a ploughshare used in the defence of a dug-out. In spite of t ... of bricks and mortar a ... tion of earth from und ... foundations of the ho ... dug-outs and machir ... placements were neve ... damaged.

It was unpleasant an ... and yet, in some sort, ... creep down the pinched ... the deeper dug-outs. Y ... to avoid kicking the n ... brush" grenades left u ... once I saw one of our N ... There was always a feel ... might come suddenly ... mate, dead or alive; an ... found even later than th ... frightened into corn ... either to fight or surren ...

As I crept up ag ... trench from one of th ... heard the machine guns ... front with some extra i ... was, I think, the mom ... final attack was pushed ... "Railway Alley" and ... Wood," just over the I ... Fricourt. The villag ... wholesome place to stay ... I had no desire to imitat ... of Marius in the ruins ... Besides, for the purpose ... progress of the battle ... better to be on the hill I ...

FLOWER-COVERED

The position of the

Creeping barrage

Communications were difficult, but it became clear that the cavalry ranks waiting to consolidate a glorious infantry breakthrough would not be needed. There had been some gains: the German line breached to a depth of a mile in places, a couple of target villages taken. The use of a "creeping barrage" – where foot-soldiers advanced behind a moving curtain of shellfire – reaped dividends where it was efficiently employed. To the south the French made encouraging progress, attaining all set targets. Their artillery bombardment was concentrated on a narrower front, and the German line facing them was more lightly defended. These were bright spots in a day that ended with almost half of the 120,000 troops deployed on the casualty list. Nearly 20,000 lay dead, for the capture of less than three square miles. It was the darkest day in the annals of British military history, but the generals were not about to allow such details to throw them off a course that had been months in the plotting.

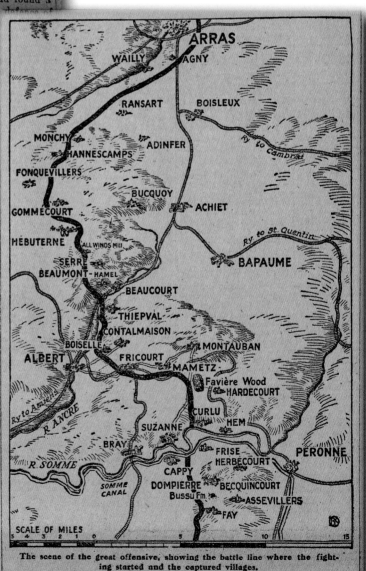

The scene of the great offensive, showing the battle line where the fighting started and the captured villages.

A large-scale map of the battle, specially prepared for The Daily Mail, appears in

CRATER CAUSED BY EXPLOSION OF A MINE JUST BEFORE THE ASSAULT

ORIGINAL BRITISH FRONT LINE

Nearly 20,000 lay dead, for the capture of less than three square miles.

Left: A series of mines prepared by the Royal Engineers were designed to destroy German defences and provide cover for the advancing Allies at the start of the offensive. The majority were blown up at 7.28 am on the first day of the Battle but failed to make any significant impact as German commanders had moved troops to the safety of their deep dug-outs.

Left and below: Within a matter of days the millions of pounds of explosives used on the battlefields resulted in complete desolation with casualties littering the landscape.

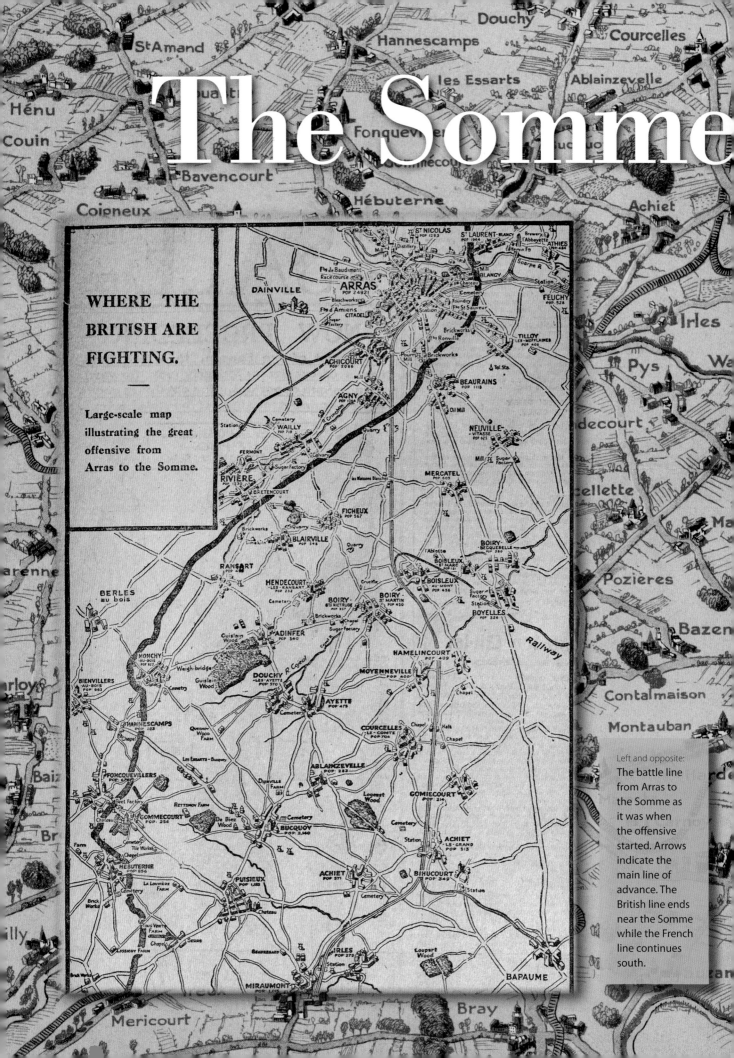

The Somme

WHERE THE BRITISH ARE FIGHTING.

Large-scale map illustrating the great offensive from Arras to the Somme.

Left and opposite: The battle line from Arras to the Somme as it was when the offensive started. Arrows indicate the main line of advance. The British line ends near the Somme while the French line continues south.

battleground

KEY MAP

SCALE OF MILES

14-mile frontline

The decision to make the sector east of Amiens astride the River Somme the point of the Allied offensive in summer 1916 was driven by the fact that this was where the British and French armies rubbed shoulders. In its original conception, the French were to lead the charge. The bloodbath of Verdun changed all that: the poilus would play a supporting role; Britain, for the first time, was to be the senior partner in a joint operation. And not before time, as far as many of France's high-ranking figures were concerned.

This area of Picardy had been relatively quiet, for there were no important strategic targets in sight. Joffre, the plan's original architect, was simply out to inflict casualties on a scale the enemy could not withstand. When Haig took the reins, the scheme developed into an attack on a 14-mile front, between Serre in the north and Maricourt in the south. There was to be a diversionary raid at Gommecourt, just above Serre, while the French Sixth Army would attack on either side of the river on a further eight-mile front. The breadth of the offensive was meant to counter the problem of flanking fire that bedevilled narrow-front assaults, but had the disastrous corollary of diluting the artillery barrage. Haig wanted to puncture the German line, with two cavalry divisions ready to exploit holes created by the gunners and infantry. The failure to entertain the prospect that the enemy might have dug deep into the chalk, negating the effects of the bombardment, set up a battle that was brutally attritional. Falkenhayn's directive that every inch of lost territory should be retaken immediately ensured that it ground on. The battle evolved into a piecemeal struggle, though Haig never abandoned hopes that these would lead, incrementally, to a dramatic outcome. Almost 100 small-scale attacks were launched in the two-month period from mid-July, delivering less than three square miles into Allied hands. The desperate need for good news prompted the BEF commander-in-chief, under fire from his political masters, to throw the newly-arrived tanks into action in mid-September. When the offensive was finally brought to a halt, the Allies had penetrated seven miles at most. French gains came at a fraction of that cost. Estimates of German casualties vary, but were high enough for Ludendorff to comment that his army "had been fought to a standstill".

Above: **French troops on the march following their defeat of the German Second Army after an attack from both sides of the Somme.**

Below: **A wounded soldier is helped to safety by a comrade. On the first day of the Somme the British suffered just under 60,000 casualties with 90 per cent of these claimed by German Maxim machine-guns.**

When Haig took the reins, the scheme developed into an attack on a 14-mile front, between Serre in the north and Maricourt in the south.

Above: **A vigilant British soldier keeps watch from the trenches, well protected by sandbags. The trenches created by the German Army were generally more elaborate and much deeper than Allied constructions. One captured on the Somme in 1916 had been fitted out with electricity, ventilation and toilets and, bizarrely, was decorated with wallpaper.**

G. R.

Your
King & Country
need another
100,000 Men.

IN the present grave national emergency another 100,000 men are needed at once to rally round the Flag and add to the ranks of our New Armies.

Terms of Service
(Extension of Age Limit).

Age on enlistment 19 to 38. Ex-Soldiers up to 45. Minimum height 5 ft. 4 ins. except for ex-soldiers and those units for which special standards are authorised. Must be medically fit. General Service for the War.

Men enlisting for the duration of the War will be able to claim their discharge, with all convenient speed, at the conclusion of the War.

Pay at Army Rates.

Married men or Widowers with Children will be accepted, and if at the time of enlistment a recruit signs the necessary form, Separation Allowance under Army conditions is issuable at once to the wife and in certain circumstances to other dependents.
Pamphlet with full details from any Post Office.

How to Join.

Men wishing to join should apply in person at any Military Barrack or at any Recruiting Office. The address of the latter can be obtained from Post Offices or Labour Exchanges.

God Save the King.

July 1916

July 1, 1916 – The Battle of the Somme began on the Western Front. The opening day of the battle saw the British Army suffer the worst single-day death toll in its history: of the nearly 60,000 British casualties that day, 18,800 soldiers were killed. Nine Victoria Crosses (six posthumously) were awarded on the first day of the battle (see page 24).

July 2, 1916 – British troops began their attack south of the road between Albert and Bapaume.
The attack to recapture Montauban from the British by the German commander, General von Below, failed and the German Army withdrew from the Flaucourt Plateau.

July 3, 1916 – After fierce fighting British troops successfully recaptured parts of La Boiselle but failed to gain ground at Ovillers and Thiepval. The French Sixth Army moved across the Flaucourt Plateau and reached the village of Flaucourt.
The Germans began to switch resources from the offensive at Verdun to defend the Somme.
Lieutenant Adrian Carton de Wiart and Private Thomas Turrall each receive the VC for their part in the fighting at La Boiselle.

July 4, 1916 – Heavy thunderstorms resulted in the first signs of the infamous Somme mud and impeded progress as British soldiers continued their advance in La Boiselle. French troops took Belloy-en-Santerre and Feuillières.

July 5, 1916 – Hem, a first-day objective for the French Army, was captured by the XX Corp. It was taken over by British troops later in the year.
Two VCs were awarded: the first to Lieutenant Thomas Wilkinson for his heroic deeds at La Boiselle; Second Lieutenant Donald Bell received the other after his actions at Horseshoe Trench near Mametz Wood.

July 6, 1916 – In a counter-attack, German troops almost succeeded in retaking Hem on the night of 6-7 July.
Major Billy Congreve was posthumously awarded the VC for his actions over a two-week period at Longueval.

Battle of Albert

The Somme Offensive can be split into a number of distinct phases, the first of which spanned the costly opening day and ran through to 13 July. The Battle of Albert, as it was known, revealed the hollow optimism of the plan to penetrate a German line crushed under the weight of the ferocious preliminary bombardment. The artillery – and heavy guns in particular – was spread too thinly, there were too many duds and insufficient high-explosive shells to inflict the kind of damage Haig hoped for. Skeleton sentry crews faced the hit-and-miss onslaught; the main body of the German Army was insulated in deep dugouts awaiting the call. The French, learning hard lessons from Verdun, adopted more flexible tactics instead of advancing in rigid lines and presenting an inviting daylight target. They made headway in the south, helped by the fact that the enemy had not anticipated a concerted strike in this area. There were also gains in the southern sector of the British front, around Fricourt and Mametz, which Haig sought to exploit in the period 2-13 July. By the end of the Battle of Albert, the British had in their sights the German second line at Bazentine Ridge, Haig having recalibrated the objective as a "wearing-out" assault – a precursor to a renewed late-summer attack – rather than a swift, decisive breakthrough.

Below: The combination of shell craters and heavy rain produced difficult terrain for men, animals and motor vehicles, including the latest battlefield weapon: the tank, which was introduced in September 1916.

Opposite above: Due to the high casualty rate in the first phase of the war, the majority of the British fighting force were now volunteers from Kitchener's Recruits and the Territorial Army. Retired soldiers and inexperienced men gained senior positions swiftly, reducing the levels of competence.

Opposite below: The southern part of the battleground. The space between the dotted line and the black line represents the ground gained by the Allies. Figures indicate height in metres. The inset map shows the line from Lille to Peronne.

The Battle of Albert revealed the hollow optimism of the plan to penetrate the German line.

for the "OVER-SEAS DAILY
every week for a year to a friend in
OF THE WORLD.

MONDAY

BIRD'S-EYE VIEW OF TH

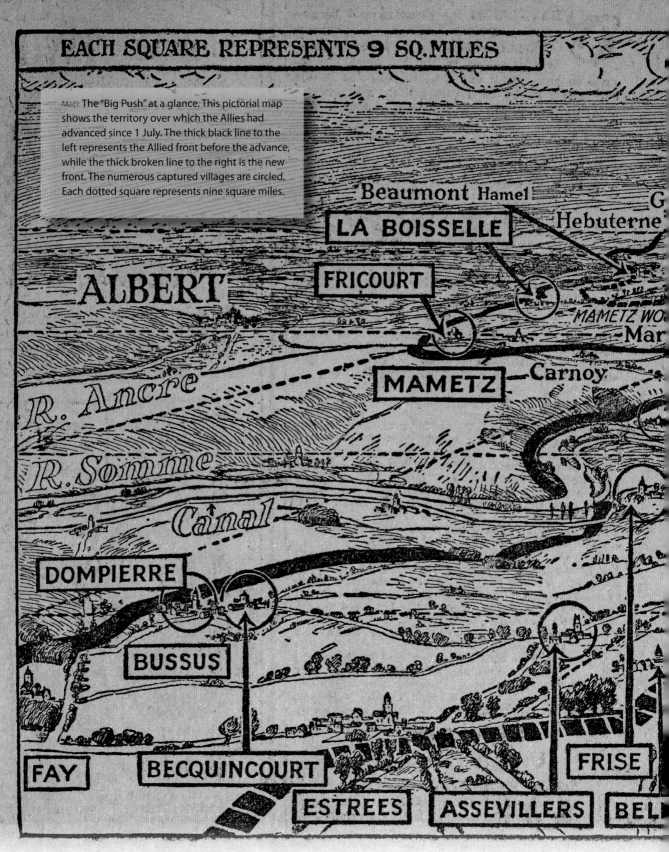

EACH SQUARE REPRESENTS 9 SQ. MILES

Map: The "Big Push" at a glance. This pictorial map shows the territory over which the Allies had advanced since 1 July. The thick black line to the left represents the Allied front before the advance, while the thick broken line to the right is the new front. The numerous captured villages are circled. Each dotted square represents nine square miles.

Beaumont Hamel

G.

LA BOISSELLE

Hebuterne

FRICOURT

MAMETZ WO

ALBERT

Mar

MAMETZ

Carnoy

R. Ancre

R. Somme

Canal

DOMPIERRE

BUSSUS

FAY

BECQUINCOURT

FRISE

ESTREES

ASSEVILLERS

BEL

SOMME BATTLE GROUND.

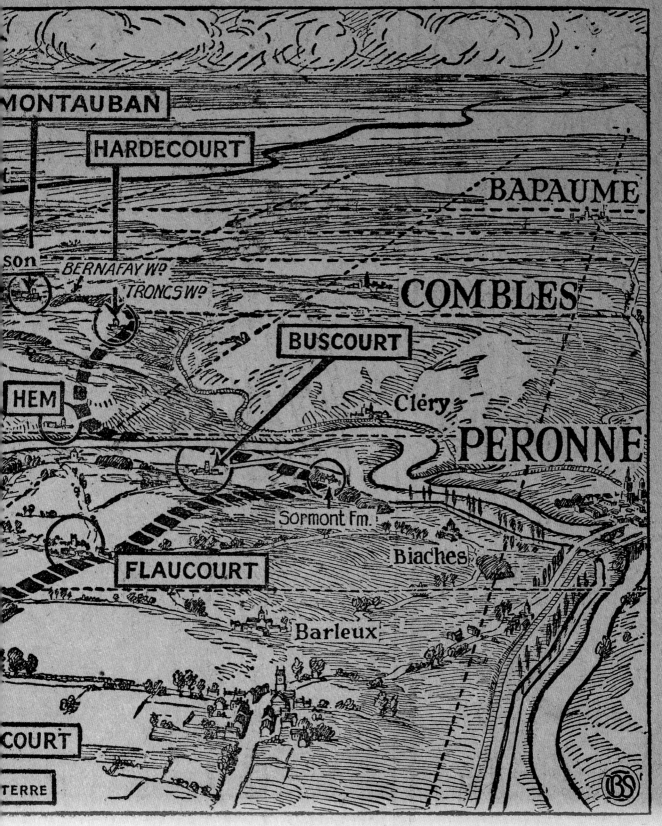

MONTAUBAN

HARDECOURT

BAPAUME

son

BERNAFAY W?

TRONCS W?

COMBLES

BUSCOURT

Cléry

HEM

PERONNE

Sormont Fm.

Biaches

FLAUCOURT

Barleux

COURT

TERRE

THE
This a
lies s
hospit

The Daily Mail," shows the country over which the British and French

BRITISH STRUGGLE IN A WIRED WOOD.

GERMAN GAIN AFTER FIVE REPULSES, BUT LOSS AT OTHER POINTS.

FRENCH STORM HILL BY PERONNE.

707th DAY OF THE WAR.
11th DAY OF ANGLO-FRENCH OFFENSIVE.

Somme Battle : After five repulses the Germans got a slight gain in the Troncs Wood, a little over a mile east of Montauban. The British made progress in the Mametz Wood, east of Ovillers, and near Contalmaison (2½ miles east-north-east of Albert), where 3 guns and several hundred prisoners were taken. A wonderful despatch from Mr. Beach Thomas describes the epic struggle at this point. South of the Somme the French have brilliantly carried a height which dominates Péronne and is less than a mile from it. Since Sunday's reports they have captured over 1,000 prisoners.

Péronne is an important junction where three lines meet, one from Montauban, a second from Chaulnes, and a third from St. Quentin and the north. The first two are under the fire of the Allied artillery.

FRENCH RUSH A HEIGHT.

POSITION THAT DOMINATES THE RIVER.

French Official. PARIS, Monday Night:

North of the Somme a quiet day. South of the river some progress during the day in the region between Biaches and Barleux and near the latter village. In the outskirts of Biaches we carried a small fort, where an enemy detachment still held out. We took 113 prisoners, including 10 officers.

South-east of Biaches by a brilliant attack we carried Hill 97 (1,500 yards south-west of Péronne), which dominates the river and had been strongly held. We also took the Maisonnette Farm on the summit and rushed a copse north of the farm. Parties of the enemy still remain in a redoubt near the extremity of the copse.

VIOLENT VERDUN FIRE.

North of Verdun the enemy artillery, vigorously countered by our guns, shelled with great violence the regions of Froide-

Below: Men of the Royal Warwickshire Regiment enjoy a well-earned sleep in the open after their part in the Battle of Albert.

Opposite above: German casualties lie abandoned in a trench taken by the Allies.

Opposite below: French poilus bring in a badly-wounded soldier. French troops originally fought in their traditional red pill-box hats, blue frock-coats and red pantaloons. However, a new blue uniform was swiftly introduced as the red was dangerously visible on the battlefield. In 1915, they also brought in their own version of the steel helmet – the Adrian helmet.

HAND-TO-HAND IN OVILLERS.

WEEK'S STRUGGLE IN A DUST HEAP.

MR. BEACH THOMAS'S DESPATCH.

From W. BEACH THOMAS.

WITH THE BRITISH ARMY IN THE FIELD,
Thursday.

In Ovillers, on the left of our advance, our troops have fought a hand-to-hand fight for a week and more, gaining ground without a set-back, though all the time till to-day the progress was measured by yards, or at most by chains. Twenty-tw yards here may mean a mile elsewhere.

Ovillers is a village with a church in the middle and many good solid houses close together. Nevertheless and notwithstanding, Ovillers has seen no street fighting, no house-to-house fighting, for the place of these things is no more seen. To-day it would trouble you to find the church or any street or any house. The village has vanished more completely than Neuville St. Vaast or Souchez, through which the old padre walked without recognising the place of his life habitation. I speak the bare fact.

Yet neither is the substitute for houses a mere dusty knoll, for, like other town-

Nine Victoria Crosses awarded on the first day

Walter Potter Ritchie

A drummer in the Seaforth Highlanders, Walter Ritchie did not escape entirely unscathed during the first two years of war, but he was in position with his fellow Highlanders for the "Big Push" on 1 July 1916.

His battalion was to be in the second wave as part of a division whose point of attack was near the village of Beaumont-Hamel, which included the German stronghold called Redan Ridge. Once the advance brigade had secured its objectives, the plan was for the 2nd Seaforths to surge forward, leapfrogging them and making deeper inroads into enemy territory, but as Ritchie and his comrades made their move, they came under withering machine-gun and artillery fire from positions still very firmly in enemy hands. The first wave had been cut to pieces, and the second threatened to be similarly decimated. As the day wore on, some of the attackers did make it to the third German line, albeit at heavy cost. Officer casualties compounded the problem, an air of rudderlessness adding to the chaos and confusion. Some of those still standing were beginning to fall back. It was at this point that Drummer Ritchie brought a semblance of calm and cohesion to the scene by mounting an enemy parapet and sounding the charge repeatedly on his bugle. A clear target to the enemy, Ritchie's example had a steadying effect in rallying the troops around him. His actions could not alter the course of the battle – the 2nd Seaforth Highlanders alone lost one-third of its strength killed or wounded, over 300 casualties – but his heroism in coming to the fore, meant Ritchie was one of nine men put forward for the Victoria Cross. His citation noted that he displayed "the highest type of courage and personal initiative", and commended him further for carrying "messages over fire-swept ground" for the entire day. Instead of being reprimanded for taking his bugle onto the battlefield, when that had ceased to be accepted practice, he received the highest award for gallantry.

George Sanders

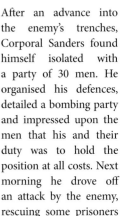

After an advance into the enemy's trenches, Corporal Sanders found himself isolated with a party of 30 men. He organised his defences, detailed a bombing party and impressed upon the men that his and their duty was to hold the position at all costs. Next morning he drove off an attack by the enemy, rescuing some prisoners who had fallen into their hands. Thirty-six hours later and after two further bombing attacks he was finally relieved of his position. All this time Sanders' party had been without food and water, having given their water to the wounded during the first night.

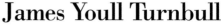

James Youll Turnbull

On the morning of 1 July 1916, Sergeant Turnbull's Battalion had gone over the top heading towards a German stronghold known as the Leipzig Salient. As the German guns opened fire hundreds of men were cut down, but Turnbull was among those who managed to reach the objective and hold it. Although his squad was wiped out, Turnbull never wavered in his determination to hold his post, throwing grenades and turning machine-guns on the enemy. He almost single-handedly maintained his position but later in the day was killed by a sniper.

Eric Norman Frankland Bell

At Thiepval Captain Bell was in command of a Trench Mortar Battery when he advanced in an attack with the Infantry. As the front line was being raked with machine-gun fire, Captain Bell crept forward and shot the machine-gunner. On several occasions later on, when various bombing parties were unable to make any progress, he went forward on his own and threw trench mortar bombs among the enemy. When he had run out of  bombs, Bell stood on the parapet under intense fire and used a rifle on the advancing Germans. He was killed whilst rallying and reorganising infantry parties which had lost their officers. As his body was never recovered, Captain Bell is remembered on the Thiepval Memorial and the nearby Ulster Memorial Tower.

William Frederick McFadzean

On 1 July 1916, near Thiepval Wood, Private McFadzean stood in a crowded concentration trench where a box of bombs was being opened for distribution prior to an attack. The box fell down into the trench and two of the safety pins fell out. Instantly realising the danger to his comrades, the private threw himself on top of the bombs which exploded instantly, blowing him to pieces, but injuring only one other man. He fully understood the danger but gave his life for his comrades without a moment's hesitation.

Geoffrey St George Shillington Cather

On the night of 1 July 1916, near Hamel, Lieutenant Cather was searching for wounded men in no man's land in full view of the enemy and under direct machine-gun fire and intermittent artillery fire. After bringing in three wounded men he continued his search and brought in another casualty and gave water to others. The next morning, he took out  water to another man and was continuing to search for others when he was killed.

John Leslie Green

At Foncquevillers, on the first day of the Battle of the Somme, and despite being wounded himself, Captain Green went to the assistance of an officer who had also been wounded and was trapped on the enemy's wire entanglements. Under heavy enemy fire, he was able to drag the other officer to a shell-hole, where he dressed his wounds. Through a hail of bombs and rifle grenades Green then tried to move him to safety but was killed before he could do so.

Robert Quigg

On the first day of the Battle of the Somme, advances by the British troops were slow and costly. Private Quigg's platoon suffered hundreds of casualties as they were beaten back three times by the Germans. As the battle raged Lieutenant Macnaghten went missing and it was Robert Quigg who immediately volunteered to search for his commander in no man's land. Under heavy shell and machine-gun fire he made seven sorties, each time bringing back a wounded man. The last man he dragged in on a waterproof sheet from within yards of the enemy's wire. After seven hours of trying, an exhausted Quigg finally gave up; the body of Harry Macnaghten was never found.

Stewart Walter Loudoun-Shand

When Major Loudoun-Shand's company attempted to climb over the parapet to attack the enemy's trenches near Fricourt, they were met by very fierce machine-gun fire, which temporarily stopped their progress. The major immediately leapt on the parapet, helped the men over it and encouraged them until he was mortally wounded. Even then, he insisted on being propped up in the trench, and went on encouraging the non-commissioned officers and men until he died.

Tragic downside of "Pals" scheme

Between the annihilation of the BEF professionals in the opening months of the war and the introduction of conscription in 1916, Britain relied on volunteers to maintain its army strength. War Secretary Lord Kitchener had led the drive to raise a New Army and fronted the famous poster campaign, urging the nation's menfolk that duty beckoned in this hour of desperate need. Lord Derby was also a prime mover in a staggeringly successful recruitment process that quickly exceeded its initial 100,000 target. For many patriotic fervour and the desire to fight for a just cause on behalf of king and country was enough. But the chance to serve with those they lived amongst or worked alongside added a spur of camaraderie to the devotional incentive. As Lord Derby put it when he addressed the men of Merseyside on 28 August 1914: "This should be a battalion of pals, a battalion in which friends from the same office will fight shoulder to shoulder for the honour of Britain and the credit of Liverpool". The rate of enlistment was such that Liverpool soon had enough men to furnish four battalions, and the idea was not slow in catching on across the land. All manner of groups – from sportsmen to stockbrokers to school alumni or simply men from the same community – grasped the opportunity to head into battle shoulder to shoulder. The make-up of these units made for immediate cohesion. They marched to the step of a shared connection; a common bond to match the common purpose. But this well-intentioned idea was to have tragic consequences for some towns and villages. Where a policy of dispersal across the regiments might have spread the casualty count, concentration of men from the same area also concentrated the losses if a pals' battalion happened to find itself in the thick of fierce fighting. Among the hardest hit were the Accrington Pals, who suffered grievously on the first day of the Somme battle.

Below: **Four VC winners from the Somme campaign pictured after receiving their medals from the King. L to R: Private JC Kerr, Corporal FJ Edwards, Private TWH Veale and Private HW Lewis.**

Opposite: **Journalist W. Beach Thomas said these Somme veterans fought with "almost ludicrous calmness".**

"This should be a battalion of pals, a battalion in which friends from the same office will fight shoulder to shoulder."

The Accrington Pals

Accrington and its neighbouring districts had been quick to answer the call, one of the smallest urban areas to muster a 1,000-strong battalion. Those who formed the 11th Battalion of the East Lancashire Regiment had a considerable wait before they were able to show their mettle. There was a lengthy period of training, and when they finally headed overseas in December 1915, it was to Egypt, part of an Allied force ready to counter any threat to the Suez Canal. By February 1916 concerns over an imminent Turkish attack had subsided and the 11th East Lancashires were redeployed to the Western Front, where plans were being laid for a large-scale summer offensive. They were anything but battle-hardened, and now were heading for a baptism of fire unparalleled in British military history.

The Accrington Pals had by now been subsumed within the 94th Brigade, 31st Division, made up of similar units from across the Lancashire-Yorkshire region. They arrived at the front line at around 3.00 am on 1 July, having undertaken an exhausting six-mile march from their rearward position, a trek begun the previous evening. It was hardly the best preparation for a battle due to begin four hours later, but that didn't matter – as long as this was the walkover everyone expected. Anything less and they faced a daunting task: taking the hilltop fortress at Serre. Defences here would have taxed the most astute generals and crack troops. The Pals lacked nothing in spirit but were ill-prepared to wrest this formidable redoubt from the German Army's 169th Infantry Regiment.

Mown down like meadow grass

Seven hundred and twenty went over the top that morning. Like all the others, they walked into no-man's-land heavily laden with kit. Like all the others, they anticipated an unhindered advance. And like all the others, they quickly found that the week-long artillery bombardment had not killed or incapacitated the enemy ranks. The dug-in German machine-gunners emerged from their sanctuaries, and the Pals were "mown down like meadow grass", in the words of one observer. To make matters worse, the preliminary shelling had been as ineffective in smashing the barbed wire as it had been in neutralising the living, breathing defence. Those who survived long enough made for the gaps, clustering in the enemy's sights. Some actually made it to the German trenches, as did some of their 94th Brigade comrades from the Sheffield Battalion to their left. There were reports that a few reached the village of Serre itself. Brigadier-General Hubert Rees, who was in temporary command of the 94th, reported: "Not a man wavered, broke the ranks or attempted to go back." He added: "I have never seen, indeed could never have imagined such a magnificent display of gallantry, discipline and determination." But the situation was hopeless, not least because the men of the 13th and 14th York and Lancaster Regiment – the 1st and 2nd Barnsley Pals that formed the second wave – were also cut to pieces. Without reinforcements, the shattered remains of the Accrington battalion had no option but to scramble back to their own trench haven. In less than an hour the toll of killed, wounded or missing stood at 584. Just 136 of the 720 who set out escaped unscathed.

Virtually every Accrington household was affected in some way, the grim news met with a blanket drawing down of blinds and incessant tolling of the church bells. It was a scene repeated in towns and cities across the land, places such as Bradford and Grimsby. For weeks the Barnsley Chronicle printed lists of the town's fallen heroes. Communities had their hearts ripped out. The most unfortunate parents might have lost more than one son. Widows and their orphaned children were left to pick up the pieces. It was too great a burden to bear, as the authorities now appreciated. The idea of "pals" marching into battle together was quietly shelved as the calamitous downside of close-knit comradeship revealed itself on the opening day of the Somme battle.

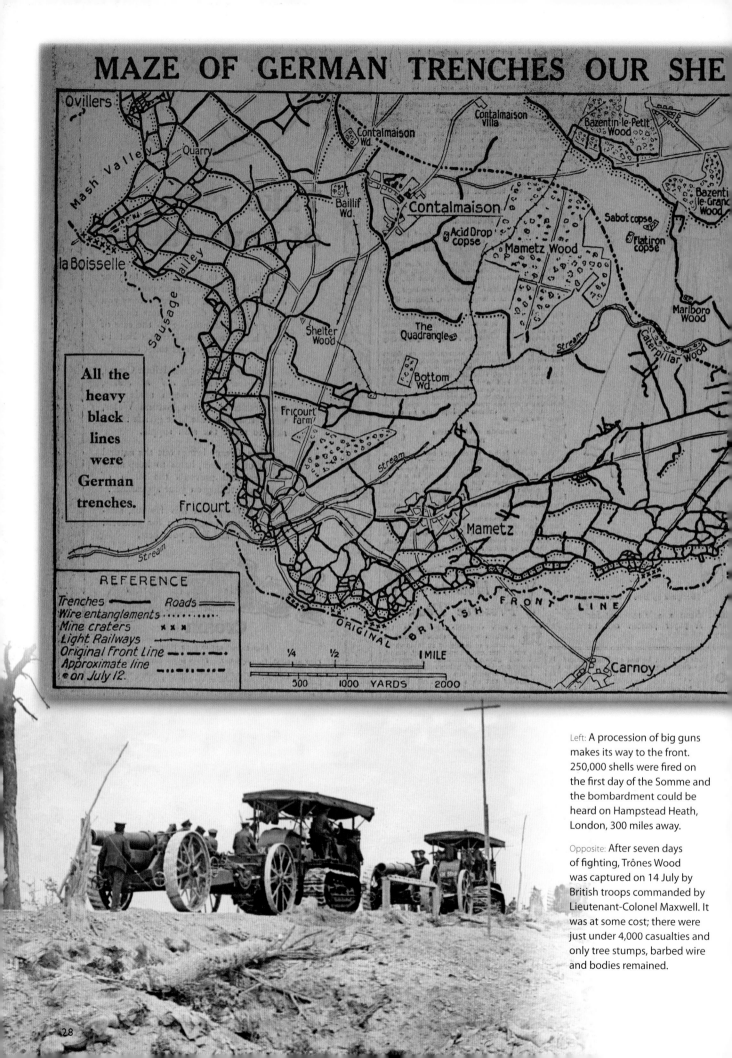

Ovillers

Contalmaison Villa

Bazentin-le-Petit Wood

Contalmaison Wd.

Mash Valley

Quarry

Bazentin-le-Grand Wood

Baillif Wd.

Contalmaison

Sabot copse

Acid Drop copse

Flat iron copse

Mametz Wood

la Boisselle

Sausage Valley

Marlboro Wood

Shelter Wood

The Quadrangle

Stream

Caterpillar Wood

Bottom Wd.

All the heavy black lines were German trenches.

Fricourt Farm

Stream

Fricourt

Mametz

Stream

REFERENCE

Trenches ━━━ Roads ═══
Wire entanglements ·········
Mine craters ✕✕✕
Light Railways ┼┼┼┼┼
Original Front Line ─·─·─·─
Approximate line ·─··─··─·
on July 12.

ORIGINAL BRITISH FRONT LINE

¼   ½   1 MILE

500   1000 YARDS   2000

Carnoy

Left: A procession of big guns makes its way to the front. 250,000 shells were fired on the first day of the Somme and the bombardment could be heard on Hampstead Heath, London, 300 miles away.

Opposite: After seven days of fighting, Trônes Wood was captured on 14 July by British troops commanded by Lieutenant-Colonel Maxwell. It was at some cost; there were just under 4,000 casualties and only tree stumps, barbed wire and bodies remained.

D MEN HAVE WON.

BROTHERS KILLED.

LORD ST. DAVIDS LOSES HIS SECOND SON.

Lord St. Davids has received news that his only surviving son and heir, Captain Roland Philipps, Royal Fusiliers, was killed in action on July 7. Captain Philipps, who was wounded in March this year, was awarded the Military Cross in April.

Lord St. Davids' elder son, Captain Colwyn Philipps, Royal Horse Guards, was killed in May last year and there is now no heir to the title.

Lieutenant Harry L. Cholmeley, Border Regiment, who was killed on July 1, aged 23, was the youngest son of Mr. L. C. Cholmeley, of Messrs. Frere, Cholmeley, and Co., of Lincoln's Inn-fields. One brother, Second-Lieutenant H. V. Cholmeley, Grenadier Guards, was killed on April 7, and the only surviving brother, Captain G. H. Cholmeley, London Regiment, was wounded on July 1.

Lieutenant P. Neill Fraser, North Staffordshire Regiment, killed, was a brother of Miss M. Neill Fraser, the Scottish golfer, who died of typhus last year in Serbia, where she was one of the Scottish nurses.

Captain A. N. S. Jackson, of the King's Royal Rifles, the famous Oxford runner who in the Olympic Games at Stockholm in 1912 established a record (3min. 56 4-5sec.) for the 1,500 metres (937 yards), was wounded in the recent fighting

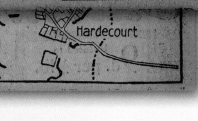

July 1916

July 7, 1916 – German troops held back a British assault on Mametz Wood, seen as a vital objective in protecting the British right flank.
David Lloyd George succeeded the late Lord Kitchener as British Secretary of State for War.

July 8, 1916 – The British capture of Trones Wood, another vital objective, was short-lived as a German counter-attack drove them out.

July 9, 1916 – The British Liberal politician Edwin Samuel Montagu was appointed Minister of Munitions in Great Britain.

July 10, 1916 – By the evening, the French Sixth Army had pierced the German third line opposite Péronne at La Maisonette and Biaches.

July 11, 1916 – The British began a bombardment of the German second line around Bazentin-le-Grand in preparation for an infantry attack on the ridge.

July 13, 1916 – British troops captured Mametz Wood and Contalmaison and broke through the German line at Bazentin Ridge, but the success of the latter was temporary as they were pushed back.

July 14, 1916 – The Battle of Bazentin Ridge began, launching the second phase of the Somme Offensive.
Longueval Ridge was captured, along with Trones Wood, at which Sergeant William Boulter's actions earned him the VC.
British forces cleared Mametz Wood, four-and-a-half km past the German lines.

July 15, 1916 – A subsidiary attack, the Battle of Delville Wood, began when South African troops attempted to clear the woods of German forces. The attack was prolonged and continued through the summer into September.

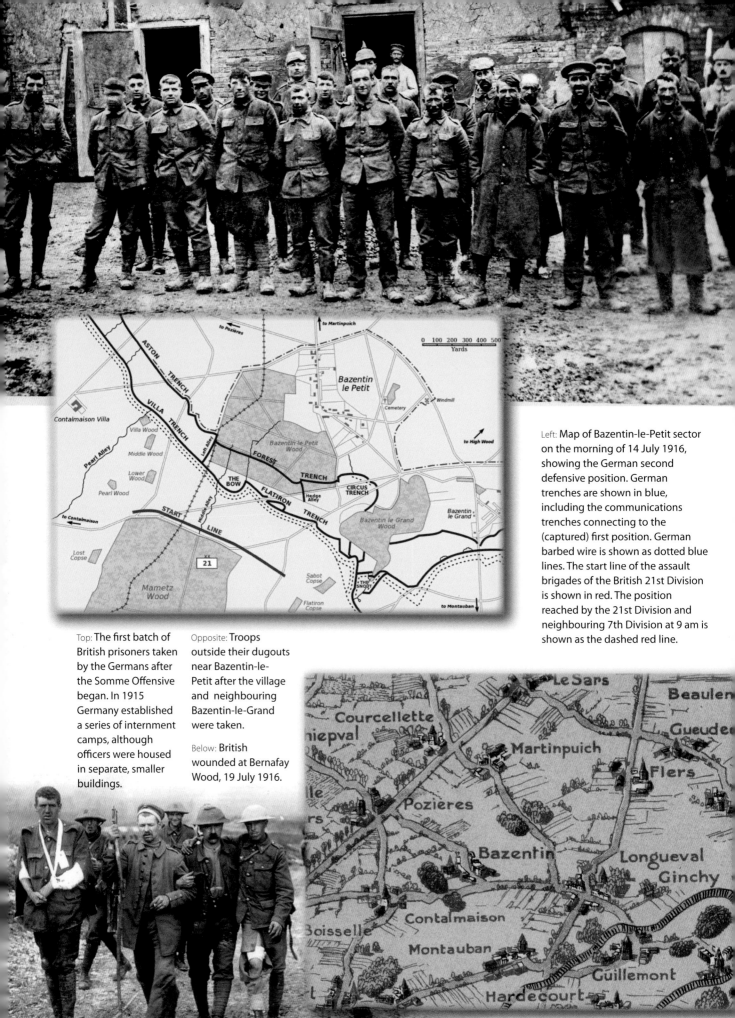

Left: Map of Bazentin-le-Petit sector on the morning of 14 July 1916, showing the German second defensive position. German trenches are shown in blue, including the communications trenches connecting to the (captured) first position. German barbed wire is shown as dotted blue lines. The start line of the assault brigades of the British 21st Division is shown in red. The position reached by the 21st Division and neighbouring 7th Division at 9 am is shown as the dashed red line.

Top: The first batch of British prisoners taken by the Germans after the Somme Offensive began. In 1915 Germany established a series of internment camps, although officers were housed in separate, smaller buildings.

Opposite: Troops outside their dugouts near Bazentin-le-Petit after the village and neighbouring Bazentin-le-Grand were taken.

Below: British wounded at Bernafay Wood, 19 July 1916.

BRITISH INTO THE SECOND GERMAN LINE.

| LAGES CAPTURED. | HAND-TO-HAND IN OVILLERS. | officer and six men found themselves alone in the extreme edge of the trench thus: | FRANCE'S FALLEN. | ARMY "VIEWERS." | THE BEST BATT ANECDOTE. |

I CARRY 2½ MILES OF SECOND GERMAN DEFENCES.

WEEK'S STRUGGLE IN A DUST HEAP.

MOVING HOMAGE.

ALLEGED BLACKMAILING OF CONTRACTORS.

PICK-A-BACK ON A

TER-ATTACKS CRUSHED.

MR. BEACH THOMAS'S DESPATCH.

THREE MILLIONS VIEW THE ALLIES' MARCH.

MR. MUIR'S STORY OF AN HONEST MAN RUINED.

OFFICER'S FIN

A "DESIRABLE" DUG-

From W. L. McALPIN.

Battle of Bazentin Ridge

General Rawlinson commanded the attack on Germany's second position at Bazentin Ridge on 14 July, an assault that brought more welcome news for the Allies a fortnight after the devastating losses incurred on the opening day of the Somme battle. The bombardment that preceded the advance was more concentrated than 1 July – fewer guns but on a significantly shorter front – and thus considerably more effective. It was a short, sharp shock rather than drawn-out pummelling, lasting only five minutes before the men moved forward. More emphasis was given to counter-battery fire, which would neutralise enemy guns once the attack was in progress. The creeping barrage, too, was better executed than had been the case in earlier phases of the battle.

Rawlinson's decision to gather his men in no-man's-land under cover of darkness – a plan Haig thought ill-advised – proved inspired. The commander-in-chief thought it too risky for inexperienced soldiers, deferring only after his 4th Army general urged him to reconsider. A 3.25 am raid and narrowing of the gap the frontline troops had to cross, in tandem with the brief artillery burst, caught the Germans off-guard, exactly as

Rawlinson had hoped. In a matter of hours the British were in possession of a 6,000-yard stretch of the enemy's second line between Bazentin-le-Petit and Longueval. Haig could barely contain his delight at the day's work. "This is indeed a very great success," he wrote, adding: "The results of today will be very far reaching."

The strategically important High Wood appeared to be within the Allies' grasp. Briefly undefended in the confusion, the door lay ajar, but the initiative was lost in a delay while the cavalry were brought up. Rawlinson was a victim of his own success, no one expecting the mounted division would be pressed into service so soon. The plan could have been amended, infantry pushing on instead of the cavalry, to whom the task had been designated. That this didn't happen was a missed opportunity in an otherwise successful operation.

The arrival of German reserves ensured that High Wood and the neighbouring Delville Wood – "Devil's Wood", as the men called it – remained in enemy hands, the struggle for mastery of those areas raging for several weeks.

HEAVY ATTACKS ON THE BRITISH.

GROUND LOST BUT MOSTLY REGAINED.

GUNS SCATTER GERMANS GATHERING FOR ASSAULT.

BRITISH OFFICIAL.

FRANCE, Wednesday.

2.10 P.M.—The enemy's attack last night, the beginning of which has already been reported, was directed against our new positions to the east of Bazentin village. Very large German reinforcements had been collected for this attack.

After an intense artillery fire the first assault was delivered in dense masses about 5.30 p.m. Fighting continued all night, and was particularly violent in Delville Wood [on the right of the four miles of the second German line in our hands].

After suffering very heavy losses the enemy recaptured a portion of Delville Wood, and also obtained a footing in the northern outskirts of Longueval [adjoining the south-western edge of the wood]. The struggle in these areas is still violent.

Elsewhere his attack, including three separate assaults on Waterlot Farm (south-east of Delville Wood), completely broke down under our fire.

On the rest of our front no event of importance has occurred.

9.30 P.M.—North of the Somme heavy fighting is still in progress in Longueval village and Delville Wood. In both these places we have already regained most of the ground lost last night.

South of Delville Wood this afternoon we dispersed with our fire a large body of Germans massing to attack Waterlot Farm from the direction of Guillemont [south-east of the farm].

FAMILY'S SACRIFICE.

TWO BROTHERS KILLED, THIRD BROKEN IN INTERNMENT.

SIR. T. EDEN'S RETURN.

Sir Timothy Eden, who has just returned to Windlestone Hall, Durham, after being interned in Germany since the beginning of the war, is confined to bed, but is progressing favourably. He was released because of ill-health.

Sir Timothy, who is 23, was completing his education in Germany when the war broke out. His father, Sir William Eden, who had the famous lawsuit with Whistler over Lady Eden's portrait, died in February last year, and as the eldest son, Lieutenant John Eden, 12th Lancers, was killed in action in October 1914, the present baronet succeeded to the title while a prisoner. Midshipman William Nicholas Eden, another brother, who was just 16, went down in the Jutland battle in the Indefatigable. Sir William's only daughter is Lady Brooke, wife of Brigadier-General Lord Brooke; Lieutenant Robert Anthony Eden, the heir presumptive, is in France.

The battle of Fromelles was a diversionary attack, intended to occupy the German line 45 miles north of the Somme.

Australian casualties alone exceeded 5,000, Germany's losses a mere fraction of that.

Below: Troops use the camouflage of a smokescreen to launch another attack.

Battle of Fromelles

The Battle of Fromelles took place some distance from the Somme, yet was integral to the overall scheme insofar as it was launched to occupy German troops in that sector, to forestall the possibility of redeployment from a perceived "quiet" zone to the thick of action some 50 miles to the south. If the German hierarchy were minded to send reinforcements to the area, so much the better.

Fromelles marked the first significant action involving Anzac troops on the Western Front. Many, including 15th Brigade commander Harold "Pompey Elliott", were Gallipoli survivors and had only recently arrived in France. There was precious little to time to acclimatise to the new surroundings when the battle orders arrived. Any who thought they had already experienced the worst the war could throw at them were soon to be disabused of that notion. This would be the archetypal baptism of fire. One would liken it to the Charge of the Light Brigade, "but more terrible, more hopeless".

This ill-fated diversionary assault on a 4,000-yard front began on 19 July and lasted just 24 hours. The central target was an imposing, elevated salient known as Sugar Loaf, from where the Germans could oversee the ground across which the attack would come. A seven-hour preliminary bombardment achieved little apart from alerting the enemy to what was afoot. The concrete bunkers housing the machine-gun emplacements survived intact, the attacking infantry cut down in waves almost as soon as they set foot into no-man's-land, which was 400m wide in places. It was grisly confirmation of one British staff officer's prediction that the enterprise would result in "a bloody holocaust".

British soldiers attacking the other side of the salient fared no better than their Aussie comrades. The sole encouraging note was struck when Anzacs managed to occupy part of the forward trench, but without support that foothold was soon lost. Australian casualties alone exceeded 5,000, the worst day in the country's military history. German losses were a mere fraction of that.

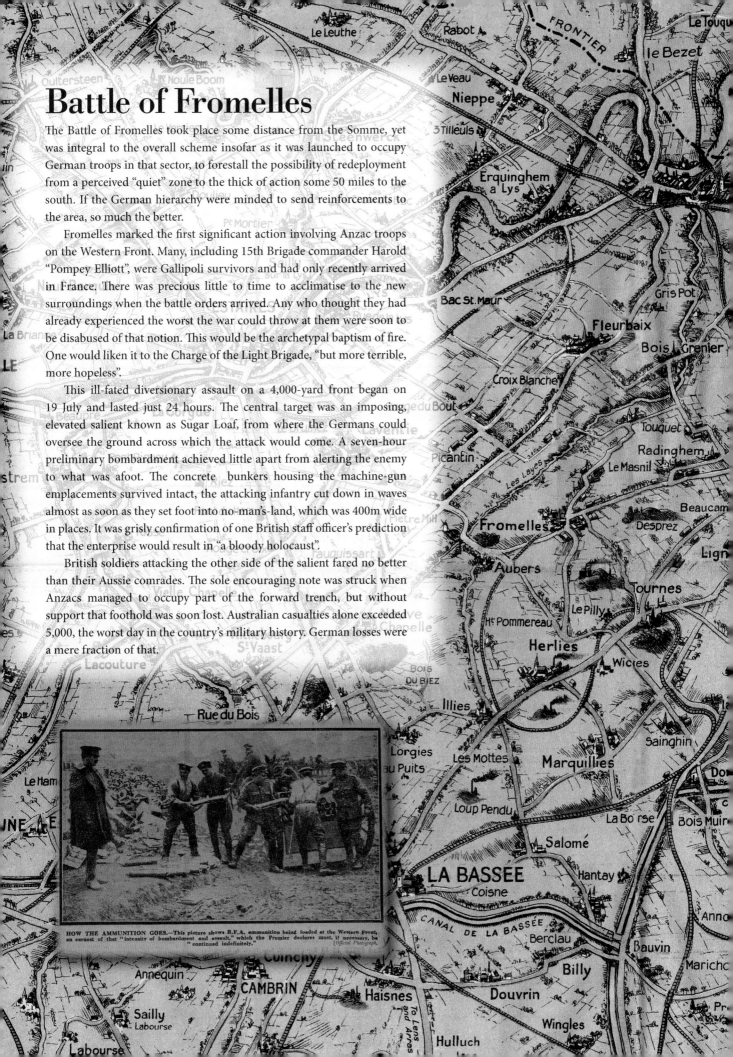

HOW THE AMMUNITION GOES.—This picture shows R.F.A. ammunition being loaded at the Western Front, an earnest of that "intensity of bombardment and assault," which the Premier declares must, if necessary, be "continued indefinitely." [Official Photograph.]

HEAVY ATTACKS ON THE BRITISH.

GROUND LOST BUT MOSTLY REGAINED.

RUSSIA'S WATCH FOR WEAK POINTS.

VOLHYNIA GUNS ACTIVE.

From HAMILTON FYFE.

PETR... Tuesday.

I said a week ago...

3 VILLAGES CAPTURED.

BRITISH CARRY 2½ MILES OF SECOND GERMAN DEFENCES.

COUNTER-ATTACKS CRUSHED.

WEST KENTS HOLD OUT 48 HOURS AND WIN.

BRITISH OFFICIAL.

FRANCE, Friday.

10:4 A.M.—This morning at dawn I attacked the enemy's second system of defence. Our troops have broken into the hostile positions on a front of four miles and have captured several strongly defended localities. Heavy fighting continues.

9.17 P.M.—It is now possible to give further details of the action begun at daybreak this morning. Having driven the enemy back step by step to his second system of defence, the period 11th to 12th July (Tuesday and Wednesday) was mainly spent by our troops in bombarding these formidable positions and in other necessary preparations for a further advance.

This morning, after an intensive bombardment, the assault was launched at 3.25 a.m. The enemy was driven from his trenches on the whole front of attack and many prisoners fell into our hands.

Fierce fighting has continued all day, as the result of which we have steadily increased our gains and are now in possession of the enemy's second positions from Bazentin-le-Petit village to Longueval village (both inclusive) and the whole of Trônes Wood.

In Trônes Wood we relieved a party of the Royal West Kent Regiment, who, separated from our own troops in the recent fighting and surrounded by the Germans, had gallantly held out in the northern end of the wood for forty-eight hours.

Two determined counter-attacks on our new positions were completely crushed by our fire. Later in the day, after a fierce counter-attack, the Germans succeeded in recapturing the village of Bazentin-le-Petit, but were at once driven out again by our infantry, and the whole village is once more in our hands.

F THEIR LOST GROUND.

ROM
S.

ELLS.

HOMAS.

ENGLISHWOMAN IN A
BERLIN CELL.

A "RETALIATION" EXCUSE.

Englishwomen are being thrown into German gaols as retaliation for the alleged im-
prisonment of German women and children
in England.

BRITISH NAMES.

THE CASE OF THE STOCK
EXCHANGE.

We publish below a list of members of
the Stock Exchange who have adopted
British names as shown in the official
members of the Stock Ex-

WAR ELECTION

REBUFF TO CABINET.

THE HOUSE DEMANDS
LEADERSHIP.

Above: A platoon of the
Worcestershire regiment in good
spirits marches to the front line.

Battle of Delville Wood

It is, perhaps, fitting that the sole memorial honouring the South African officers and men who fell on the Western Front was constructed at Delville Wood. For it was here that the South African Brigade distinguished itself, and suffered appalling losses, as the Allies sought to build on the success of the attack on Bazentin Ridge.

Two weeks' fighting had left the Allies with a reasonable grip on the village of Longueval, through which the German second line ran. The next target was the adjacent forested area, since enemy forces ensconced here would have threatened the Allied rear. Three thousand South African troops went into action as part of the 9th (Scottish) Division, tasked with making the initial assault on 15 July. The area, rechristened "Devil's Wood" by the men who fought there, was a hell-hole of chaos, confusion and bloodletting. After six days of battle, during which time South African troops had to withstand withering German counterattacks, the Brigade had lost three-quarters of its complement. Heavily outnumbered, they were further hampered by the terrrain: shattered and fallen trees made trench construction difficult, and protection thus tended to be shallow and rudimentary. Torrential rain added to the misery, turning the battlezone into a morass. Relief finally came, and the fight for Delville Wood went on as the valiant, much-depleted South African forces counted the heavy cost.

Haig had the cavalry on stand-by, thinking this could be their moment at last. That optimism evaporated as the opposing forces fought bitterly over ground reduced to matchwood. At the height of the battle seven shells rained down on the same benighted patch of earth every second. In a 24-hour hurricane bombardment on 18 July – before the South African infantry were relieved – German artillery hit a square-mile target with 20,000 shells. The advantage swayed back and forth before Delville Wood was eventually secured by the Allies in the first week of September, though it would change hands again before the Armistice was signed.

Delville Wood was eventually secured in the first week of September, though it would change hands more than once before the guns fell silent.

Below and opposite above: The strategically important Delville Wood was soon renamed "Devil's Wood" by British soldiers. At the height of the battle, German shells rained down at a rate of 400 a minute, resulting in almost total deforestation.

LONDON SCOTTISH MARCHING

THE LONDON SCOTTISH AGAIN.—Remembered for their charge in the early days of the war, the London Scottish have again distinguished themselves. In the advance of July 1 they performed feats that earned for them high praise in a Divisional Order issued by the general commanding. He said: "I wish to express to all ranks my supreme admiration of the conduct of the battalion in the action of the 1st inst. The great traditions of which we are all so proud were maintained and added to, while the individual

Left and bottom: Delville Wood marked the first major involvement on the Western Front of the South African First Infantry Brigade, under the command of Brigadier-General Henry Lukin. After a ferocious six-day battle only 750 of the 3,000-strong South African force survived to see relief troops arrive. Despite their losses the South African troops managed to hold onto the wood.

Below: The pipes and drums of the Black Watch played to the troops after the initial capture of Longueval.

"England Expects . . . ."

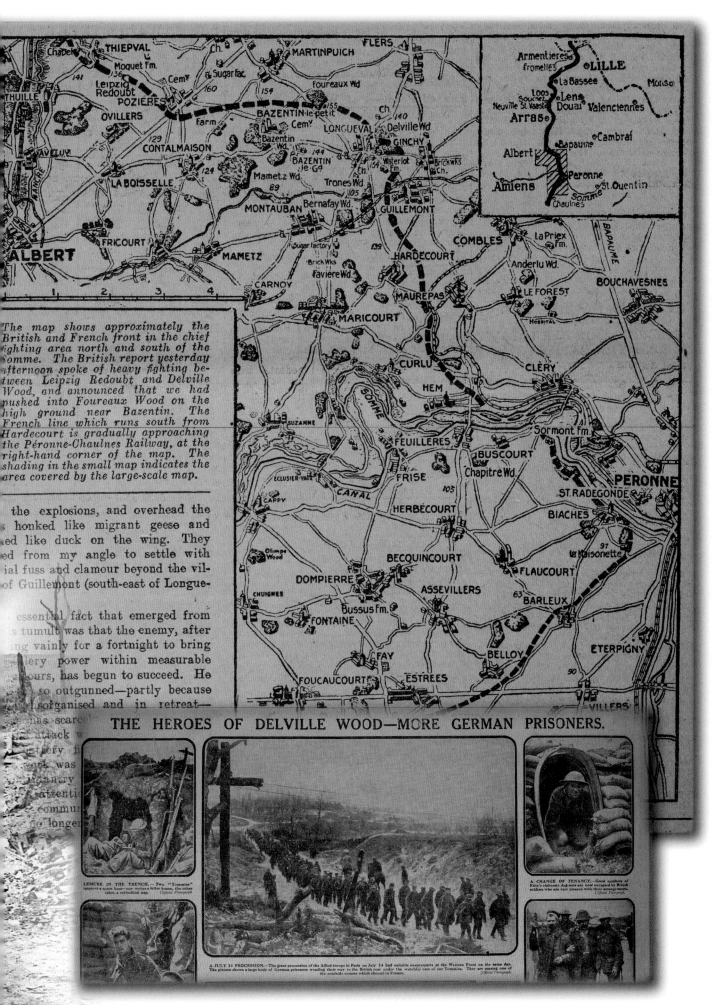

THIEPVAL · Chapel · Moquet Fm. · 136 · Ch. · MARTINPUICH · FLERS
Sugar Fac. · Cem? · 160 · 154 · Foureaux Wd. · Ch. · 140
THUILLE · Leipzig Redoubt · 141 · POZIÈRES · 155 · Delville Wd.
OVILLERS · Farm · BAZENTIN-le-petit · Cem? · LONGUEVAL · GINCHY
AVELUY · 129 · CONTALMAISON · Bazentin Wd. · 144 · BAZENTIN · le-Gd · Ch. · 154 · Waterlot Fm. · Brickwks · Ch.
LA BOISSELLE · 124 · Mametz Wd. · 89 · Trones Wd. · 105 · GUILLEMONT
ALBERT · FRICOURT · MAMETZ · MONTAUBAN · Bernafay Wd.
Sugar Factory · 139 · HARDECOURT · COMBLES · La Priex Fm.
Brick Wks · Anderlu Wd.
CARNOY · Faviere Wd. · 13 · MAUREPAS · LE FOREST · BOUCHAVESNES
Hospital
MARICOURT · CURLU · CLÉRY
HEM · SOMME · Sormont Fm.
SUZANNE · FEUILLERES · BUSCOURT
ECLUSIER-VAUX · FRISE · Chapitre Wd. · PERONNE
CANAL · 103 · ST. RADEGONDE
CAPPY · HERBÉCOURT · BIACHES
Olimpe Wood · BECQUINCOURT · 97 · la Maisonette
DOMPIERRE · FLAUCOURT
CHUIGNES · ASSEVILLERS · 63 · BARLEUX
Bussus Fm. · FONTAINE · BELLOY · ETERPIGNY
FAY · ESTRÉES · 90
FOUCAUCOURT · VILLERS

Inset map:
Armentieres · fromelles · LILLE
La Bassée · Mons
Loos · Souchez · Lens · Douai · Valenciennes
Neuville St. Vaast · Arras
Cambrai
Albert · Bapaume
Péronne · St. Quentin
Amiens · Somme
Chaulnes

The map shows approximately the British and French front in the chief fighting area north and south of the Somme. The British report yesterday afternoon spoke of heavy fighting between Leipzig Redoubt and Delville Wood, and announced that we had pushed into Foureaux Wood on the high ground near Bazentin. The French line which runs south from Hardecourt is gradually approaching the Péronne-Chaulnes Railway, at the right-hand corner of the map. The shading in the small map indicates the area covered by the large-scale map.

the explosions, and overhead the [...] honked like migrant geese and [...]ed like duck on the wing. They [...] from my angle to settle with [...]ial fuss and clamour beyond the vil-[...] of Guillemont (south-east of Longue-[...]

[...] essential fact that emerged from [...] tumult was that the enemy, after [...] vainly for a fortnight to bring [...]llery power within measurable [...]ours, has begun to succeed. He [...] so outgunned—partly because [...] organised and in retreat—[...] has scarce[...] attack w[...] [...]ntery f[...] [...]k was [...]fantry [...] attenti[...] commun[...] [...] longer[...]

THE HEROES OF DELVILLE WOOD—MORE GERMAN PRISONERS.

LEISURE IN THE TRENCH.— Two "Tommies" improve a spare hour—one writes a letter home, the other takes a refreshing nap. [Official Photograph.]

A JULY 14 PROCESSION.—The great procession of the Allied troops in Paris on July 14 had suitable counterparts at the Western Front on the same day. The picture shows a large body of German prisoners wending their way to the British rear under the watchful care of our Tommies. They are passing one of the roadside crosses which abound in France. [Official Photograph.]

A CHANGE OF TENANCY.—Great numbers of Fritz's elaborate dug-outs are now occupied by British soldiers who are very pleased with their arrangements. [Official Photograph.]

BRITISH NEARING THE RIDGE FO

GROUND WON IN POZIÈRES.	**MACHINE GUNS.**	**FRENCH CAPTURE A REDOUBT.**	**PETROL RATI**
USTRALIANS IN CONTINUOUS FIGHTING.	GERMAN "ROOKERY" AT POZIÈRES.	**VERDUN PRISONERS.**	DISTRIBUTING F ALARM.
VERY HEAVY GERMAN LOSSES	ENEMY TROOPS FROM MANY		SERIOUS THREAT TO
LLOYD GEO		nday Night. Infantry cap- west of the of Verdun). risoners were	Petrol has become a gre problem. It is one of the prim of industry, and the great red
MANY			

The SMOKE of BATTLE

**WILLS'S
10 GOLD FLAKE
for 4D CIGARETTES**

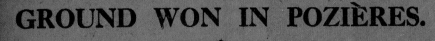

IN TURKEY.

THEIR PROPER ~ATMENT.

Government has been misled by the conspicuous being accorded to ~d into thinking that the men, prisoners of the ~n comfort.

have not been afforded whatever to inquire into ~der which our prisoners Mesopotamia are living, ~lly unjustified that their to be desired.

~y and honours which his ~king on General ~ ~arsal trick of ~

IRISH BREAKDO~

MR. REDMOND WARNS GOVERNMENT.

NATIONALISTS G~ INTO OPPOSITIO~

SIR E. CARSON'S GREAT A~

MR. ASQUITH ON FATE ~

By OUR PARLIAMENTARY REPRES~

Opposite above: Troops take advantage of the water collected in shell-holes to have an early morning wash.

Below: A well-earned breakfast for members of the Black Watch.

GROUND WON IN POZIÈRES.

AUSTRALIANS IN CONTINUOUS FIGHTING.

VERY HEAVY GERMAN LOSSES.

MR. LLOYD GEORGE ON OUR GREAT RESOURCES IN MEN.

MANY MORE BIG GUNS AND SHELLS WANTED.

BRITISH OFFICIAL.

FRANCE, Monday.

12.6 P.M.—Apart from continuous heavy shelling by both sides a night of comparative calm followed the severe fighting of yesterday.

Yesterday, between High Wood [the Foureaux Wood] and Guillemont the repeated counter-attacks of the enemy gained for him no advantage, and very heavy casualties were inflicted by our artillery and machine-gun fire. We have gained some ground near High Wood and in the direction of Guillemont.

In the neighbourhood of Pozières our troops have secured important advantages, in spite of the stubborn defence of the enemy, and a large portion of the village is now in our hands.

In this neighbourhood we have captured 2 guns and 60 more prisoners.

9.43 P.M.—Fighting has continued in the village of Pozières, where the number of prisoners taken by the Australian troops has reached a total of 6 officers and 145 other ranks.

In other parts of the battle-front there has been considerable artillery activity on both sides.

Between the Ancre and the sea nothing of importance has occurred.

721st DAY OF THE WAR.
25th DAY OF ANGLO-FRENCH OFFENSIVE.

Battle of the Somme: The fighting shows no diminution in fury, though it has now reached its 25th day. With the exception of the Battle of Verdun, which has lasted for five months, this is the severest struggle in this war of fearful and prolonged encounters, and it has been glorious to British arms.

The first ten days of infantry fighting, from July 1 to 10, witnessed our capture of the enemy's whole first system of defences on a front of 14,000 yards and to a depth of 2,000 yards. On July 11 and 12 the enemy's second line was severely bombarded. Our troops then attacked it, in the second phase of the battle, on a front of four miles, and by the 14th had broken into it at several points. By the 15th they had reached Foureaux, or High Wood, which is of great tactical importance, because it commands the neighbouring country.

FRENCH TAKE A BATTERY.

60 MACHINE GUNS CAPTURED SINCE THURSDAY.

French Official. PARIS, Monday Night.

South of the Somme in a small operation we captured this morning an enemy battery south of Estrées.

Since Thursday last we have taken on the Somme front more than 60 German machine guns.

Afternoon.

On the Somme front the night was quiet. The weather continues bad.

MR. LLOYD GEORGE'S REVIEW

GENERALS MORE THAN SATISFIED.

Mr. Lloyd George, speaking in the House of Commons last night as Secretary for War, said the question of making the best use of

July 1916

July 17, 1916 – The Battle of Bazentin Ridge ended in a tactical British victory, with the capture of the German second line over a front of nearly 5.5km.

July 18, 1916 – Delville Wood was temporarily captured by the South African Infantry. Private William Faulds earned his VC for his actions there and became the first South African of the Great War to receive the medal for valour.

July 19, 1916 – The Battle of Fromelles, a combined operation by British and Australian troops designed to divert attention from the main battle, began.

July 20, 1916 – The Battle of Fromelles ended with a decisive German victory and the cost of more than 5,000 Australian casualties.
Corporal Joseph Davies and Private Albert Hill earned VCs for their part in the fighting at Delville Wood; Private Tommy Veale received his medal for his actions at High Wood.

July 23, 1916 – The Battle of Pozières began. The French village, sitting on a ridge overlooking the Somme, was a vital objective for the Allies, and although the Australian and British Divisions succeeded in capturing most of it on the first day, there followed a two-week struggle to maintain their position in the village and on the surrounding ridge. The Germans made three unsuccessful attempts to retake the position on the first day.
Two Australians, Second Lieutenant Arthur Blackburn and Private John Leak, each received the VC for their part in the fighting at Pozières.

July 24, 1916 – Australian troops captured the remaining part of Pozières as the British repelled a German counter-attack at High Wood and Guillemont. By doing so, the Allies had been able, over a two-day period, to advance more than three miles along a six-mile stretch of the front.
Private Thomas Cooke was posthumously awarded the VC for his actions on the second day of The Battle of Pozières.

Top: A labour battalion build a road over captured ground. During 1916, the recruitment of men to maintain roads, railways and provide a network of support to the troops gradually became more formalised, using conscientious objectors or those not medically fit for battle.

Above: An officer receives information by wireless and gives the order to open fire. At the beginning of the war the Government took control of part of the Marconi Company; operators were swiftly trained when commanders realised the advantages of delivering messages by wireless.

Opposite middle: The Royal Garrison Artillery in action firing two 8-inch Howitzers in the Fricourt-Mametz Valley. The Allies used over 400 heavy guns at the Somme, one for every 60 yards of the front on which the attack took place.

Opposite top: With the increasing use of trench warfare and the introduction of the tank, cavalry troops were used less and less. The last major cavalry charge took place on High Wood at the start of the Somme campaign. They successfully forced some Germans to surrender but at the cost of 100 men and 130 horses.

Opposite bottom: A group of soldiers load a heavy trench mortar, more commonly known as a "flying pig" among the British troops. These tubes were ideally suited for trench conditions; missiles were fired straight into the air and fell down over the enemy.

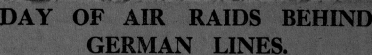

DAY OF AIR RAIDS BEHIND GERMAN LINES.

BRITISH PILOTS BLOW UP A TRAIN AND FIRE A SHELL DEPOT.

FRENCH REPEL ALL ATTACKS.

SERIOUS ENEMY LOSSES AND NO GAIN.

728th DAY OF THE WAR.
32nd DAY OF ANGLO-FRENCH OFFENSIVE

Battle of the Somme : Our troops have held all the ground gained and have made a slight advance at some points. The French have repulsed a series of terrific counter-attacks by the enemy north of the Somme, and have inflicted serious losses. Our Allies held all their new ground.

To-day's casualty lists contain the names of 273 officers and 3,793 men.

Russian Front : The battle continues furiously in Volhynia. The Russians have crossed the Stokhod east of Kovel on a front of 19 miles at least and have captured a whole Hungarian regiment (if at full strength, 3,200 men) at one point, and at another about 1,000 men. Berlin alleges that our Allies have been driven back on the Lower Stokhod and have lost 1,900 prisoners. If so, the Germans on the Lower Stokhod are now

BRITISH OFFICIAL.

10.15 P.M.—There has been no infantry fighting on the British front to-day and no incident of importance has occurred.

The Royal Flying Corps have carried out several bombing raids and dropped 7 tons of bombs on the enemy's communications and billets.

In one case a train was blown up; in another an ammunition depot was set on fire and a hostile aeroplane on the ground was destroyed.

There were many aerial combats and several enemy machines were driven to the ground in a damaged condition. Three of our machines are missing.

1.40 P.M.—Last night was spent in improving the positions gained yesterday, and there were no further de-

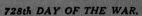

The shading indicates the ground gained between Thiepval and Peronne since July 1. Yesterday afternoon the French reported violent fighting near Monacu Farm and Hem, while the British were active north of Bazentin.

RED CROSS WORK AT THE FRONT.—LIFE IN THE TRENCHES.—FIGHTING FACES.

The R.A.M.C. IN THE FIELD.—This great service, in which our soldiers have boundless faith, is here represented doing the field work which a fortnight ago earned it the special thanks of the Commander-in-Chief. Those who know it best at home and abroad are loudest in its praise, and a young officer recently said that in tending the wounded the bearers and ambulance men seemed to say to themselves, "These King's soldiers are our comrades who have fought and suffered. The best we can give is their due." The picture shows a line of field ambulances taking up wounded near a captured village.

Top: **Gordon Highlanders** on the march with a wounded German soldier on a makeshift stretcher.

Left: **Troops remain** in the safety of their trench as they wait for the order to advance.

FAILURE OF GERMAN ATTACK ON POZIÈRES.

MOST OF THE VILLAGE NOW OURS.

THREE ENEMY ATTEMPTS AT OTHER POINTS BROKEN.

FIERCE HAND-TO-HAND FIGHTING.

BRITISH OFFICIAL,

FRANCE, Tuesday.

1.49 P.M.—During the last few days the enemy has brought further reinforcements of infantry and guns to the Somme front.

Throughout yesterday the hostile bombardment was fairly continuous and at times became very heavy. An attempt to attack our right flank was made yesterday afternoon but was frustrated by our artillery fire.

Last night two further infantry attacks, preceded by specially violent artillery fire, were launched against the centre of our line. These attacks also were stopped by the concentrated fire of our guns and rifles. At no

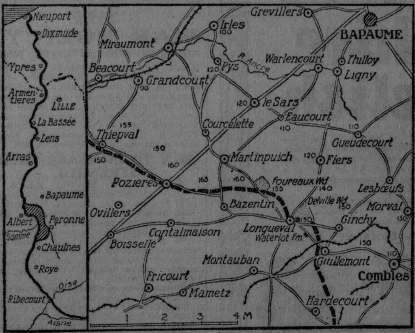

place did the enemy succeed in reaching the British trenches, and his casualties in these fruitless attacks must have been severe.

In other parts of the line there has been a good deal of hand-to-hand fighting and our infantry have worked their way forward in places.

North of Pozières, the greater part of which village is now in our possession [on the left of the battle front], the enemy continues to offer strong opposition, but here also we have gained some ground and have captured 2 machine guns and a few more prisoners, including 2 battalion commanders.

July 1916

July 25, 1916 – As the Australians cleared the remaining German troops from Pozières, a joint Anglo-French attack was agreed by Haig, Foch, Rawlinson and Fayolle for 30 July.

July 26, 1916 – At Pozières, Australian troops responded to heavy shelling from the Germans with a counter-barrage. Believing the Anzacs were about to attack, the German bombardment increased, resulting in heavy Australian casualties and the further destruction of the village, which by the end of the battle had been razed to the ground.

July 27, 1916 – At Delville Wood and Longueval, British troops shelled enemy positions. Outgunned and exhausted, a substantial number of German troops surrendered.
Sergeant Albert Gill received a posthumous VC for holding up the German advance at Delville Wood with the remains of his platoon.

July 28, 1916 – British troops captured Delville Wood and Longueval village and progressed towards Pozières. For bringing back wounded comrades in the face of intense fire on the Pozières Ridge, Sergeant Claude Castleton was posthumously awarded the VC.

July 30, 1916 – The first combined Franco-British aerial operations took place on the Western Front.
Company Sergeant Major George Evans received the VC for actions at Guillemont. He was taken prisoner the same day and released at the end of the war.

July 31, 1916 – Private James Miller earned his posthumous VC at Bazentin-le Petit on the night of 30-31 July when he ran a vital and urgent message from the trenches back to those orchestrating the battle. Despite being struck by a bullet almost immediately, he delivered the communication and returned with a reply before collapsing and dying.

Battle of Pozières

Pozières, a village lying on the Albert-Bapaume road, was one of the opening-day battle objectives that failed to materialise. There lay some of the highest ground of the entire Somme battlefield, and with strongpoints including an enemy position called "Gibraltar", the Allies were keen to wrest control. Several attempts to take these heights had been repulsed when, on 23 July, three weeks after it was meant to have fallen, Australian troops led yet another advance. The fight to capture and hold the ridge upon which Pozières stood, part of the German second line, was brutal and bloody.

The Anzacs in the vanguard of the engagement barely had time to draw breath after arriving at the front before they were hurled into the fray. Though the initial advance went well, that, as usual, represented only half a job done. Taking ground was one thing, rebuffing the inevitable enemy counter attack was quite another. The 1st Australian Division paved the way, advancing on Pozières on a two-kilometre front in the early hours of 23 July. They lost some 5,000 men, mainly to German shelling, before relief came. The 2nd Division then carried the attack, also taking heavy casualties. The 4th Division were handed the reins and to them fell the final victory, which came at the end of two weeks' sustained fighting. Both Pozières village and the ridge were in Allied hands by 7 August, German forces at last calling off their attempt to reclaim lost territory. It was another hard-won victory, but efforts to push on towards Mouquet Farm – opening the way to Thiepval – met stern German resistance.

At the end of the operation the Anzac casualty count stood at 23,000, including a death toll approaching 7,000. The losses were not far short of those incurred in the entire Gallipoli campaign. It is said the experience left the Aussies with a deep distrust of Mother Country commanders. As one private put it: "Without doubt Pozières was the heaviest, bloodiest, rottenest stunt that ever the Australians were caught up in."

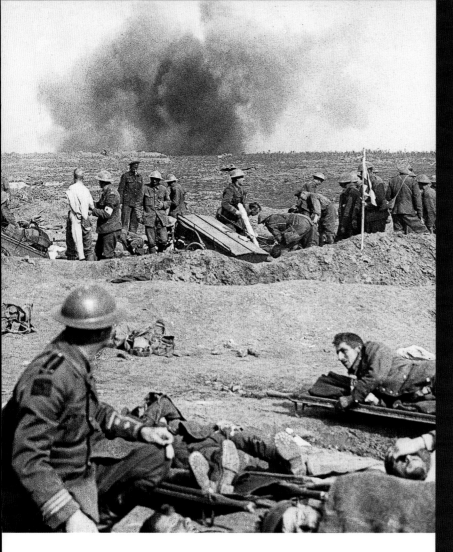

August 1916

August 1, 1916 – Allied troops repelled a German attack north of Bazentin-le-Petit; an enemy counter-attack west of High Wood also failed.

August 2, 1916 – At Pozières Australian troops continued to push forward north of the village, whilst a German attack on Delville Wood was repulsed.
Hottest day at the Battle of the Somme, temperatures reaching 88°F.

August 3, 1916 – British troops gained further ground west of Pozières.
The Irish Nationalist Sir Roger Casement was hanged at Pentonville prison for his involvement in the Easter Rising in Dublin earlier in the year.

August 4, 1916 – North of Pozières, the second German line system was captured by the British over a front stretching for almost two kilometres. Several hundred prisoners were taken.

August 6, 1916 – Private William Short gained his VC at one of the attacks on Pozières. At Munster Alley he was at the forefront of the action, bombing German positions when he was cut down by a shell and died of his wounds.

August 7, 1916 –The final German attacks were held back by Australian troops and no further enemy attempts were made to retake the village and the ridge. Anzac casualties for the battle reached around 23,000, although Lieutenant-General Sir Launcelot Kiggell, Chief of the General Staff in France under Haig, wrote to Rawlinson, Commander of the British Fourth Army on the Somme, suggesting that reports of British casualties had been exaggerated at home.
As a prelude to the Battle of Guillemont, British troops attacked the outskirts of Guillemont, north of the Somme. At the same time, soldiers of the French Army advanced north of the village of Hardecourt.

Top: A German shell bursts close to an advanced dressing station.

Below: Groups of soldiers watch British shells explode in and around the village of Pozières.

Opposite bottom: By the time the battle was over, the village of Pozières was completely destroyed. Buildings were reduced to rubble and the Australians had suffered 23,000 casualties. Unlike some French villages that suffered a similar fate and were left as memorial sites, Pozières was rebuilt and the Australian flag always flies overhead as a memorial to these men.

The casualty count stood at 23,000, a toll said to have left the Australians with a deep distrust of Mother Country commanders.

A HERO'S GRAVE.—The graves of British soldiers buried on the battle-field are carefully tended from the first by their comrades. In the picture a soldier is seen heaping white stones neatly round the wooden cross which marks such a resting-place. [Official Photograph.

48

Opposite top: Two British soldiers are buried on the battlefield while the Padre reads the solemn words of the burial service.

Opposite below: Highlanders at the front line march to the accompaniment of bagpipes.

Opposite inset: The grave of a fallen soldier is tended by a comrade.

Below: Dead soldiers lie abandoned in the trenches. At times unofficial truces were organised to allow the dead and wounded to be collected from no-man's-land. On these occasions stretcher bearers showing the Red Cross flag would recover the men, sometimes swapping the enemy dead for their own troops.

Left: British and French troops find time to entertain local children.

DELVILLE WOOD TRIUMPH.

12 HOURS' UNBROKEN FIGHTING.

MACHINE-GUN HEROISM.

TWO SMALL GAINS.

Bad weather has prevented any considerable British operation on the Somme. One or two small gains have been made, in which prisoners have been taken.

From W. BEACH THOMAS.

WITH THE BRITISH ARMY IN THE FIELD, Monday.

Delville Wood—for ever famous as Devil's Wood in the annals of many regiments—is now wholly within our lines, and we have had four days for the investigation of its every corner. I wonder whether it is understood how clever and courageous a feat of arms was the final capture, the sequel to a five weeks' struggle. The state of the wood is, of course, indescribable and is best left undescribed. Much of the fight is as little describable, because it consisted for a while of an artillery storm and nothing else. After very heavy fire the enemy, probably by accident, opened one of his very intensest bombardments with 8in. shells and the 5.9 just about the time fixed for the attack, and neighbouring troops who started later than those within the wood bore this for an hour while waiting for their chance to "go over." They were highly tested and highly triumphed.

This page and opposite: King George V, a keen supporter of the troops, visited the Western Front several times, and on one occasion broke his pelvis when a horse rolled on top of him. He had previously served in the Royal Navy but was forced to end his service when he became second in-line to the throne following the death of his older brother, Albert, in 1892.

The King on the Somme battlefield

The King returned yesterday from another visit to the front. The following is the General Order to the Army in France which his Majesty sent to General Sir Douglas Haig:-

Officers, N.C.O.s, and men.

It has been a great pleasure and satisfaction to me to be with my Armies during the past week. I have been able to judge for myself of their splendid condition for war and of the spirit of cheerful confidence which animates all ranks, united in loyal co-operation to their Chiefs and to one another.

Since my last visit to the front there has been almost uninterrupted fighting on parts of our line. The offensive recently begun has since been resolutely maintained by day and by night. I have had opportunities of visiting some of the scenes of the later desperate struggles, and of appreciating to a slight extent the demands made upon your courage and physical endurance in order to assail and capture positions prepared during the past two years and stoutly defended to the last.

I have realized not only the splendid work which has been done in immediate touch with the enemy – in the air, under ground, as well as on the ground – but also the vast organisations behind the fighting line, honourable alike to the genius of the initiators and to the heart and hand of the workers. Everywhere there is proof that all, men and women, are playing their part, and I rejoice to think their noble efforts are being heartily seconded by all classes at home.

The happy relations maintained by my Armies and those of our French Allies were equally noticeable between my troops and the inhabitants of the districts in which they are quartered, and from whom they have received a cordial welcome ever since their first arrival in France.

Do not think that I and your fellow countrymen forget the heavy sacrifices which the Armies have made and the bravery and endurance they have displayed during the past two years of bitter conflict. These sacrifices have not been in vain; the arms of the Allies will never be laid down until our cause has triumphed.

I return home more than ever proud of you.

May God guide you to Victory.

George R.I.

Ammunition for the "Big Push"

The regulars of the British Expeditionary Force were cut down at an alarming rate in the early months of war. Along with the need to address the manpower issue, the government faced a worrying shortfall in the supply of munitions. By spring 1915 the crisis was such that daily quotas for the number of rounds issued had to be imposed. Lloyd George, given responsibility for dealing with the shell shortage, was appointed munitions minister in the new Asquith-led coalition. It fell to him to mobilise the nation's resources and increase capacity. That meant taking on recalcitrant trade unionists more accustomed to capping output and resisting "dilution" – using unskilled labour in automated processes. Skilled male workers were exempted from active service, but to keep that number to a minimum women were employed in factory roles usually the preserve of men. By the end of the war almost one million women were employed in munitions work. During the five-day preparatory bombardment on the Somme the British artillery fired more than 1.5 million shells, more than in the first year of the war and another 250,000 shells were fired on 1 July.

By the end of the war almost one million women were employed in munitions work.

Above and below: During the "shell crisis" of 1915, it was widely believed there was a shortage of artillery shells getting to the front line. This lack of ammunition for the troops and the failed naval attack on the Dardanelles was blamed on the Liberal government; after a Cabinet split Prime Minister Asquith formed a coalition with the Conservative party to strengthen his position. David Lloyd George was appointed to the newly-created post of Minister of Munitions and swiftly resolved the issues.

Opposite above right and opposite below: Workers busily producing large shells at two munitions factories in France. One located in Le Creusot (below) and the other in Champagne-sur-Seine (above).

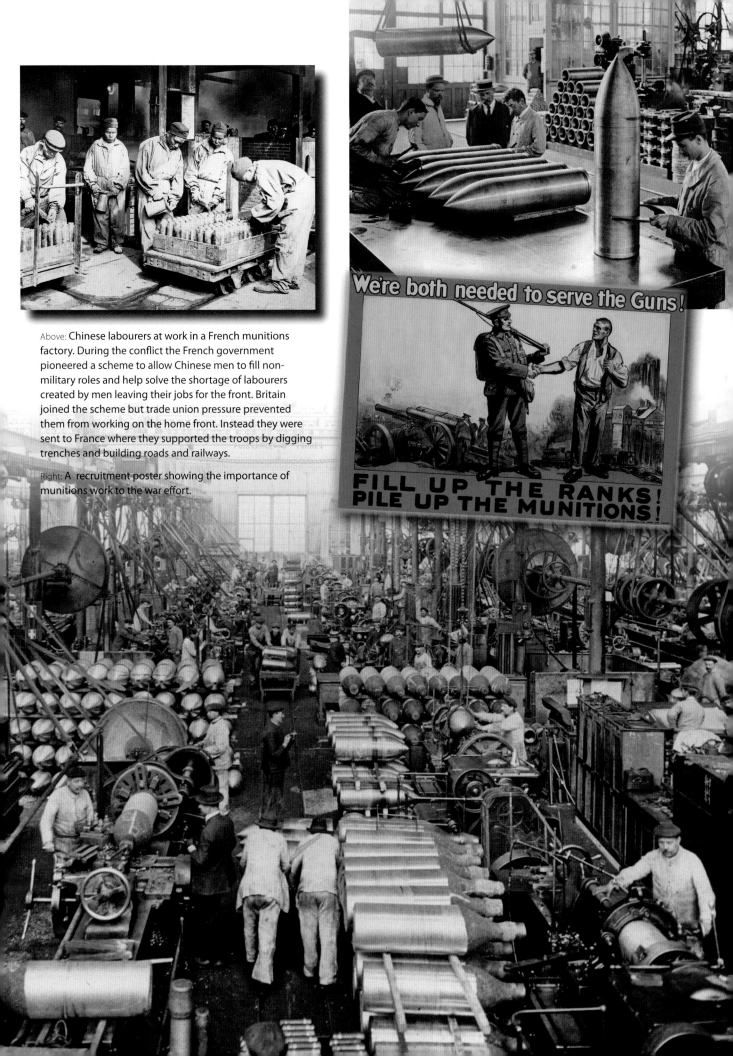

Above: Chinese labourers at work in a French munitions factory. During the conflict the French government pioneered a scheme to allow Chinese men to fill non-military roles and help solve the shortage of labourers created by men leaving their jobs for the front. Britain joined the scheme but trade union pressure prevented them from working on the home front. Instead they were sent to France where they supported the troops by digging trenches and building roads and railways.

Right: A recruitment poster showing the importance of munitions work to the war effort.

We're both needed to serve the Guns!

FILL UP THE RANKS!
PILE UP THE MUNITIONS!

Life in the trenches

When the war of movement ground to a halt and the armies dug in, commanders and foot soldiers both faced alien conditions. For the leaders it was a question of how to break the stalemate. For the infantry it was a matter of dealing with the privation and daily grind of trench life. Even for those fortunate enough to dodge a bullet or shell there was much hardship. As the months turned into years waiting for a breakthrough, the men had to endure considerable physical discomfort, while the psychological pressures told on some more than others.

The distance between the opposing lines varied along the front, no-man's-land reduced to a few metres in some places. Soldiers lived in constant fear of shellfire and snipers. Significant casualties were inflicted on men ensconced in trenches and rudimentary dugouts that offered little protection against shrapnel or the elements. Yet there were also long periods of non-engagement, time given over to routine maintenance and inspections, eating and ablutions, rest and recuperation. There was monotony as well as mayhem. At dawn and dusk – the commonest time for attacks to be launched – the men were ordered to "stand to" and placed on high alert. A "mad minute" of rapid fire might ensue. Most were then stood down, unless on fatigues or sentry duty.

Linked networks

The forward or fire trenches were divided into bays. Long straight runs were avoided to mitigate the effects of any explosion, or enemy fire if the line was breached. The trenches were around two metres deep and built up above ground level at both front and rear to give added protection. The parapet was on the enemy side, while the raised earthworks at the back of the trench was called the parados. By standing on a step men could shoot over the top of the parapet, or through a "loophole". Behind these advanced positions were the support and reserve trenches, the entire network linked by communications trenches that facilitated the movement of men and provisions, invariably under cover of darkness. There were also shallower sap trenches stretching into no-man's-land, from which enemy activity might be observed at closer quarters. The whole was a maze of thoroughfares, which were given names such as Oxford Street and Lovers Lane.

In terms of calorie intake the soldier did not fare too badly, but there was little variety in the rations. Corned beef – or bully beef – was a staple, along with bread and biscuits, tea and jam. Cigarettes at least were plentiful, and many whiled away the hours chain-smoking. There was also a daily tot of rum, dispensed by one of the NCOs.

Lice caused trench fever, a debilitating illness necessitating a lengthy period of convalescence.

Below: Much of the time in the trenches could be spent playing the waiting game. In between battles officers drew up rotas to ensure a balance of duties, sleep and rest time, but this inevitably led to boredom as soldiers waited for orders.

Health hazards

The concentration of so many men in such a confined space inevitably presented a sanitation problem. Notwithstanding the efforts of those assigned to latrine duties and attempts to disinfect the area where men lived cheek by jowl using chloride of lime, open sewers and decaying corpses created a terrible stench. They also brought rats in droves. As one veteran recalled: "The knowledge that the gigantic trench rats had grown fat through feeding on the dead bodies in no-man's-land made the soldiers hate them more fiercely than almost anything else." The reviled creatures spread infection and bred in such numbers that taking pot shots at them had little effect on the population. Lice, nits and ticks were no less of an infestation problem. Men ran candle flames over their clothing to rid it of unwanted guests. Eggs were difficult to dislodge from the seams, however, and body heat provided ideal incubation conditions. Lice were not just an irritation; they also caused trench fever, a debilitating illness necessitating a lengthy period of convalescence. It took time for doctors to discover how that disease was transmitted; frostbite and exposure were easier to diagnose, and trench foot also had a simpler causal connection. Protracted submersion in cold water and mud made the lower limbs liable to fungal infection that in the most severe cases could turn gangrenous and require amputation. The duckboards laid down on the trench floor were intended to provide a firm, dry footing above ground, but in heavy rain they did not always give adequate protection. Bitter winter temperatures and broiling summer heat brought different health hazards, before the enemy had fired a shot.

Below: **A German trench periscope doubles as a field glass.**

Above: **Soldiers quietly wait for the Padre inside a trench church which has been dug out from the side of a parapet by the poilus.**

Bottom: **A sketched plan of a German dug-out – found at Fricourt and drawn by a British officer – clearly shows how well-designed and deep they were.**

Below left: **Infantry in the trenches prepare for a gas attack. A mix of phosgene and chlorine was often used on the Somme, with the chlorine providing the vapour to carry the phosgene. This combination became known as "White Star" after the markings painted on the shells.**

55

Camaraderie in the trenches

Troops manned the various trenches on a rotation basis. After a few days on the forward line they would usually be withdrawn to the support and reserve trenches, and if there was no urgent situation, a short period of rest further from the front brought welcome respite. Here, understandably, they let off steam in predictable ways, including alcoholic binges and visiting brothels. Venereal disease in the ranks was no small problem.

Any misfortune that rendered a soldier unfit for duty, be it from shell or infirmity, meant an incremental depletion in frontline resources. Medical staff were under pressure to patch up the problem – physical or psychological – and return men to the fray. Soldiers, for their part, came to realise that a non-life-threatening condition had its compensations. "Blighty wound" entered the army lexicon for injuries that could result in a man being invalided home. Officers were on the lookout for any suspicious injury that might have been self-inflicted, an offence that carried severe disciplinary penalties.

If there was a crumb of comfort in the infantryman's lot, it came from the knowledge that adversity was a collective experience. Hardship forged deep bonds of friendship and a strong sense of camaraderie. Trench life was hellish, but at least it was a shared hell.

Opposite above: **For four years the Belgian Army successsfully guarded the Allied sector between Nieuwpoort and Ypres but did not have the military strength to assist in any major offensives.**

Right: **While German officers pore over maps and plans in a hillside trench, several soldiers write letters home. Meanwhile, the sentinel posted on the edge of a ridge closely watches the opposite hill and intervening valley for any sign of attack.**

Opposite below: **Snug holes built into the sides of an Allied trench provide a welcome resting spot for weary soldiers.**

Below: **Men of the London Rifle Brigade wait for orders.**

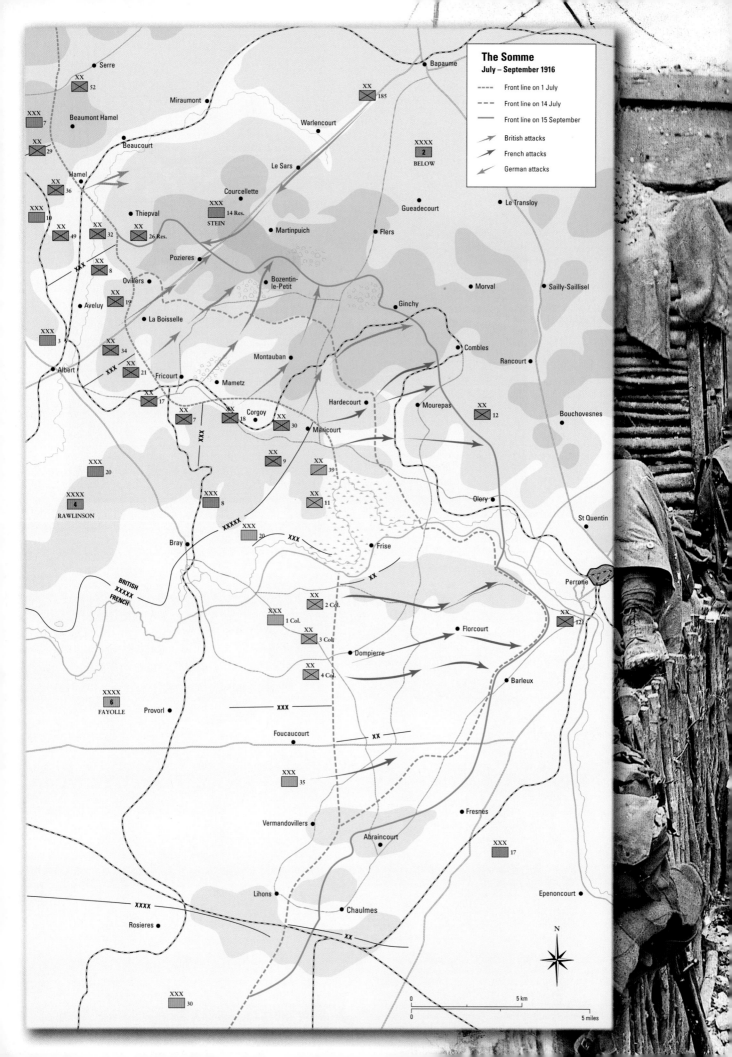

The Somme
July – September 1916

Front line on 1 July
Front line on 14 July
Front line on 15 September
British attacks
French attacks
German attacks

Serre
XX 52
XXX 7
Beaumont Hamel
XX 29
Hamel
XX 36
XXX 10
XX 49
XX 32
XX 26 Res.
XXX 8
Ovillers
XX 19
Aveluy
La Boiselle
XXX 3
XX 34
Albert
XXX 21
XX 17
XX 7
Fricourt
XX 18
XX 30
XXX
XX 9
XXX 20
XXXX 4
RAWLINSON
XXX 8
XXXXX
Bray
BRITISH
XXXXX
FRENCH
XXXX 6
FAYOLLE
Provorl
Miraumont
Beaucourt
Thiepval
XXX 14 Res.
STEIN
Courcellette
Le Sars
Martinpuich
Pozieres
Bozentin-le-Petit
Montauban
Corgoy
Mametz
Maricourt
XX 39
XX 11
XXX 20
XXX
Frise
XX
XX 2 Col.
XXX 1 Col.
XX 3 Col.
Dompierre
XX 4 Col.
Foucaucourt
XX
XXX 35
Vermandovillers
Abraincourt
Lihons
Chaulmes
XXXX
Rosieres
XXX 30

Bapaume
Warlencourt
XXXX 2
BELOW
Gueadecourt
Le Transloy
Flers
Ginchy
Combles
Rancourt
Morval
Sailly-Saillisel
Hardecourt
Mourepas
Bouchovesnes
XX 12
Olery
St Quentin
Perrone
XX 121
Florcourt
Barleux
Fresnes
XXX 17
Epenoncourt

0   5 km
0   5 miles

N

Main picture: A soldier from the Cheshire Regiment is posted on look-out duty while his comrades rest in a captured German trench in Ovillers-la-Boiselle.

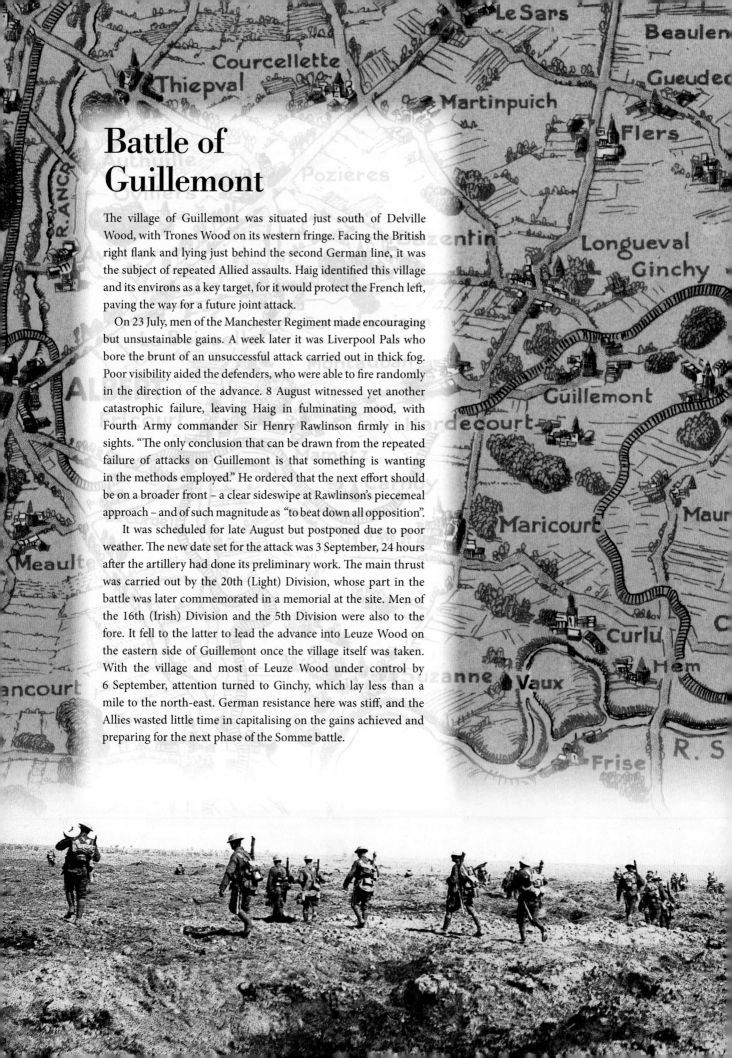

Battle of Guillemont

The village of Guillemont was situated just south of Delville Wood, with Trones Wood on its western fringe. Facing the British right flank and lying just behind the second German line, it was the subject of repeated Allied assaults. Haig identified this village and its environs as a key target, for it would protect the French left, paving the way for a future joint attack.

On 23 July, men of the Manchester Regiment made encouraging but unsustainable gains. A week later it was Liverpool Pals who bore the brunt of an unsuccessful attack carried out in thick fog. Poor visibility aided the defenders, who were able to fire randomly in the direction of the advance. 8 August witnessed yet another catastrophic failure, leaving Haig in fulminating mood, with Fourth Army commander Sir Henry Rawlinson firmly in his sights. "The only conclusion that can be drawn from the repeated failure of attacks on Guillemont is that something is wanting in the methods employed." He ordered that the next effort should be on a broader front – a clear sideswipe at Rawlinson's piecemeal approach – and of such magnitude as "to beat down all opposition".

It was scheduled for late August but postponed due to poor weather. The new date set for the attack was 3 September, 24 hours after the artillery had done its preliminary work. The main thrust was carried out by the 20th (Light) Division, whose part in the battle was later commemorated in a memorial at the site. Men of the 16th (Irish) Division and the 5th Division were also to the fore. It fell to the latter to lead the advance into Leuze Wood on the eastern side of Guillemont once the village itself was taken. With the village and most of Leuze Wood under control by 6 September, attention turned to Ginchy, which lay less than a mile to the north-east. German resistance here was stiff, and the Allies wasted little time in capitalising on the gains achieved and preparing for the next phase of the Somme battle.

Above: Welsh Guards resting in the trenches at Guillemont.

Opposite and below: Infantry exposed to enemy fire on the open ground of the battlefield. The area around Guillemont was a maze of German underground tunnels and dug-outs, adding to the dangers faced by Allied troops.

"The only conclusion that can be drawn from the repeated failure of attacks on Guillemont is that something is wanting in the methods employed."

Above: An armoured motor-car and an ambulance pull in alongside rows of stretchers.

Right: British gunners watch German prisoners being escorted away.

ALL LONGUEVAL AND DELVILLE WOOD TAKEN.

DEFEAT OF THE BRANDENBURGERS.

HAND-TO-HAND FIGHTING NEAR POZIÈRES.

GREAT ARTILLERY ACTIVITY.

BRITISH OFFICIAL.

10.15 P.M.—Continuing their successes of yesterday our troops have captured the last enemy strongholds in Longueval [on the right of the battle front], together with a number of prisoners, and in the vicinity of Pozières hand-to-hand fighting has continued throughout the day.

Elsewhere on the battle front there has been considerable artillery activity on both sides.

Two hostile aeroplanes were destroyed by one of our aerial patrols in the neighbourhood of Bapaume yesterday.

1.30 P.M.—After severe fighting our troops have driven the 5th Brandenburg Division from their remaining positions in Delville

The British front from Thiepval to Guillemont, where severe fighting continues. Yesterday the capture of Delville Wood and last strongholds of Longueval was announced.

Wood [adjoining Longueval to the north-east], capturing 3 officers and 158 men.

The whole of the wood is now in our hands and two German counter-attacks have been beaten off with heavy loss to the enemy.

We have made further progress in Longueval village and near Pozières, and in the latter area have captured 48 wounded Germans.

Last night the enemy guns were active against our new positions and there were heavy artillery duels in various sectors of the battle area.

Near Neuve Chapelle small parties of Germans succeeded in entering our front trenches at two points, but were at once driven out by a counter-attack, leaving a few wounded in our hands. North-east of Souchez and at several other points our artillery shelled the enemy's front line and communication trenches.

August 1916

August 8, 1916 – Second Lieutenant Gabriel Coury was in command of two platoons near Arrow Head Copse around the village of Guillemont when he rescued his commanding officer under intense fire and in full view of the German trenches. He was awarded the VC for his brave actions.

August 9, 1916 – French troops drove back German soldiers and advanced north of Hem Wood on the northern bank of the Somme River.

A Zeppelin raid attacked Hull on the east coast of Britain, killing up to ten people and injuring 20 more.

In an attack at Guillemont, Captain Noel Chavasse won the first of his VCs for his remarkable acts of bravery in rescuing comrades from the battlefield and dealing with numerous casualties. The bar to his VC came almost a year later at Passchendaele, but he never lived to receive it, dying a few days later from his horrific wounds.

August 10, 1916 – King George V began a 5-day tour of the Front escorted by Sir Henry Rawlinson, Supreme Commander at the Somme.

August 12, 1916 – As British troops continued to advance near Pozières, the French made gains from the Somme to Hardecourt.

At Beauquesne, Field Marshal Haig, Marshal Joffre, Commander-in-Chief of the French forces on the Western Front, and Marshal Foch met to discuss and agree a plan for a general attack on August 18 along a line of some 15km, from the Somme River to High Wood.

As part of his visit, George V met with the President of France, Raymond Poincaré.

Over a period of four days of very heavy fighting at Pozières, Private Martin O'Meara brought in wounded officers and men under intense fire, for which he was awarded the VC.

August 1916

Battle of Ginchy

The taking of Guillemont, to be followed by the nearby village of Ginchy, were key precursors to the next planned set piece: driving forward to Flers-Courcelette. Haig wanted the latter Anglo-French operation to be underway in mid-September, thus there was little room for resting on laurels following the clearing of Guillemont. Three days later, 9 September, the attack on Ginchy was launched.

Night assaults had proved their worth earlier in the battle, but here the tactics were altered. The early hours of the day were given over to the artillery to make their presence felt; it was almost 5 pm before the infantry made their move. This was designed to negate the possibility of a major enemy counter before nightfall. However, as the foot soldiers swung into action, it soon became apparent that the bombardment had missed its mark in many places, and that undisturbed enemy soldiers were ready and waiting for the onrush.

Progress was far from uniform, but 16th (Irish) Division made crucial headway and accomplished their goal in a matter of hours. It was no easy task to hold what had been won, the rebuffing of the German counter that followed adding to the steep price already paid. Over 4,000 casualties were added to the Somme account by the time Ginchy was taken.

Haig was buoyed by the success, however, entertaining hopes that the mid-September breakthrough remained on course, and that his beloved cavalry might finally be pressed into service. The capture of Ginchy had opened the door to Flers-Courcelette, the largest engagement since the battle opened on 1 July.

Opposite left: **The battlefield grave of an unknown British soldier in Ginchy is marked by his cap and rifle.**

Below: **The Battle of the Somme evolved into a piecemeal struggle, though Haig never abandoned hopes that small gains would lead, incrementally, to a dramatic outcome.**

Opposite right: **A desolate image shows French and German trenches extending close to each other with German dead lying on the small patch of no-man's-land in between.**

MAGNIFICENT FRENCH GAIN LAST NIGHT.

BREAKING THROUGH BARBED WIRE.—This striking picture shows French troops advancing over uneven ground through the barbed wire entanglements which in modern war are the most trying of obstacles and one of the worst of death-traps. Note the dreary and formidable vistas of stakes carrying the wires.
[From the "New York Tribune.

August 1916

August 29, 1916 – Field Marshal von Hindenburg replaced General Falkenhayn as Germany's new Chief of the General Staff. General von Ludendorff was appointed the Chief Quartermaster-General.

The number of German prisoners captured by the British since the beginning of the Somme offensive on 1 July was reported as: 266 officers and 15,203 men.

The Hindenburg Programme was launched; the German Supreme Army Command took control of most of the country's economy including munitions production, the labour force and food distribution as part of a policy to significantly increase the production of munitions.

August 30, 1916 –Turkey declares war on Romania.

August 31, 1916 – German troops attacked along the line between Ginchy and Bois Foureaux near the village of Pozières.

The Albatros D-series, a German fighter aircraft which would go on to give Germany air superiority, came into service. With synchronised machine-guns and twice the fire power of any Allied aircraft, it became the most powerful aircraft yet launched by the German air force.

The British casualty figures of the Great War for August alone were one-fifth of the total war dead so far.

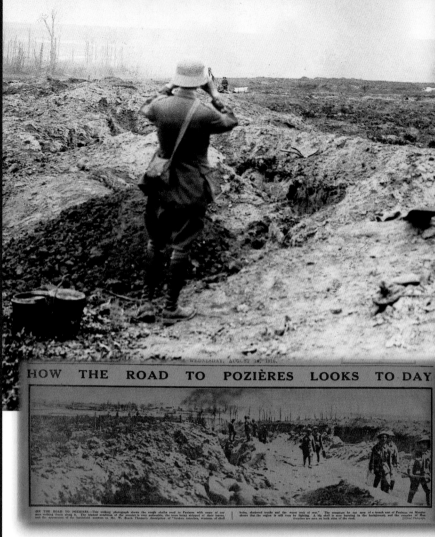

HOW THE ROAD TO POZIÈRES LOOKS TO DAY

BRITISH LABOUR BATTALION AT THE FRONT

Top: A British officer watches as German trenches near Leuze Wood are shelled. Troops soon renamed it "Lousy Woods".

Bottom: Australian troops quickly captured the village of Mont St Quentin at the beginning of September. Commander John Monash had ordered them to "scream like bushrangers" as they attacked.

Opposite below: The bodies of dead German soldiers lie scattered on the battlefield.

Opposite inset: Anti-aircraft gunners spot a German plane and lose no time in sighting and aiming their gun.

One inch to the mile map of the Thiepval-Guillemont front indicating approximately the new battle-line on the high ground north of Pozieres from which our troops look down into enemy trenches east and north-east. Guillemont quarry is shown. Figures indicate heights in metres.

Battle of Flers-Courcelette

"Certainly some of the tanks have done marvels! And have enabled our attack to progress at a surprisingly fast pace."

Thus wrote Sir Douglas Haig on 15 September, the day the Battle of Flers-Courcelette began. At the first opportunity he personally congratulated Colonel Ernest Swinton, the architect behind these new mechanical marvels, which it was hoped would give the Allies the edge. They came in male and female form, according to the weaponry carried, but more important than the firepower was their ability to override barbed wire and cross trenches. Haig wanted production ramped up so that as many tanks as possible could be put at his disposal.

So-called "land ships" – tank was merely the codename – would undoubtedly have their day and would be an important addition to an army's arsenal. But this was an encouraging debut rather than an instrument to deliver an immediate knockout blow. For one thing, they had arrived at a trickle. Instead of the 1,000 Haig had pressed for, just 32 of these armour-plated, tractor-driven vehicles were ready for action on the morning of 15 September. On a six-mile front, it meant they were scarcely entering the field en masse. Susceptibilty to mechanical failure was another issue. Indeed, there was a school of thought that the tank should have been held back until available in much greater numbers, but the need to see what they could do in the field was pressing. "This is a vital battle," wrote one of HQ's top brass, "and we should be in error to throw away anything that might increase our chance of success."

There was early encouragement in the centre with the capture of Flers by the 41st Division, where the Allies' secret weapon played its part. Rawlinson had ordered that the preliminary bombardment left lanes unshelled; unobstructed pathways to make the tanks' progress as speedy as possible – though even then they were slow and lumbering.

The swift occupation of Flers was helped by the fact that resistance was relatively light. Some enemy troops fled in the face of the metal monster, others surrendered. Meanwhile, at Courcelette in the west, the Canadians were in occupation of the village by the end of the day, though at significant cost. Martinpuich, another German stronghold, also fell, and the Allies wrested control of High Wood. To the south, however, the French fared less well.

Overall, despite the greatest territorial gain for the Allies since 1 July, the week-long engagement brought no game-changing breakthrough. Haig was no nearer the major breach in the German line he had hoped for and was coming under increasing political pressure to deliver.

"This is a vital battle and we should be in error to throw away anything that might increase our chance of success."

Right: An ammunition truck struggles to cope with the lunar-type landscape.

Above: A wounded soldier receives a welcome helping hand.

Left: The Wiltshire Regiment cross a piece of open ground.

Below: The periscope, which played a life-saving role in the First World War, was often quite short so it could be easily carried around.

HIGH EXPLOSIVE SHELL BURSTING

ENEMY TRENCHES

FRONT LINE OF FRENCH TRENCHES

"NO MAN'S LAND" AND GERMAN DEAD

THE OPPOSING TRENCHES AND "NO MAN'S LAND."—This singularly graphic picture shows the French and German trenches extending close to each other. Between them is the long sinister strip of "No Man's Land" with German dead lying here and there upon it. Other German trenches can be seen as white lines and patches on the level plain beyond; on the horizon a high-explosive shell is bursting.—*French Official Photograph.*

NEW SOMME OFFENSIVE

FRENCH AND BRITISH SUCCESSES.

GUILLEMONT AND CLERY TAKEN.

TWELVE GUNS AND OVER 2,000 PRISONERS.

FRENCH OFFICIAL.

PARIS, Sunday Evening.

To the north of the Somme, after intense artillery preparation, the French infantry, in conjunction with the British Army, attacked shortly before midday the German positions on a front of about 4 miles between the region north of Maurepas and the river with admirable dash against which the resistance of the enemy was unable to hold out for a moment.

Our troops swept away the large forces of the enemy and carried all the objectives in view.

The villages of Forest, to the east of Maurepas, and Cléry-sur-Somme are entirely in our hands.

To the north of Forest we have cap-

BRITISH OFFICIAL.

FRANCE, Monday.

12.30 A.M.—In co-operation with the French on our immediate right we attacked the enemy to-day at several points. We have captured part of Ginchy and the whole of Guillemont. Our front now runs some 500 yards east of Guillemont from Ginchy to near Falfemont Farm.

On the east side of Mouquet Farm we have also gained ground. We have captured several hundred prisoners.

Between our right and the Somme the French have made substantial progress and captured a considerable number of prisoners. Fighting continues.

Our aircraft did most useful work in co-operating with the artillery and in-

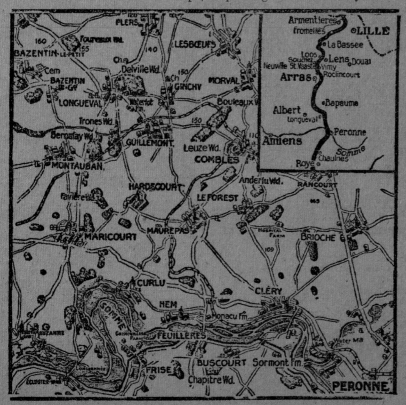

tured all the German trenches along the route from Forest to Combles as far as the outskirts of the latter place.

Between Forest and Cléry-sur-Somme we have also carried all the enemy positions. We have crossed at numerous points the road which connects these two places.

fantry. The enemy's aeroplanes, which made desperate attempts to interfere, were successfully engaged in many aerial fights and driven off with a loss of three machines destroyed and at least four others damaged, while we lost three.

FRENCH VERDUN GAIN.

September 1, 1916 – In response to Romania's aggression against Austria-Hungary, Bulgaria declared war on its northern neighbour and invaded in the form of the Danube Army.

German troops failed to secure High Wood but moved in again on the eastern side of Delville Wood.

September 2, 1916 – Fourteen Zeppelins raided England, dropping bombs from Gravesend, east of London, to Peterborough. One Zeppelin was shot down over London by a British aircraft.

Lieutenant Commander of the British Fourth Army, Sir Henry Rawlinson, showed disappointment in the standards of training and handling when he inspected the new armoured tanks, which would be used for the first time at the Battle of Flers-Courcelette.

September 3, 1916 – The Battle of Guillemont began as the British advanced and secured the village but failed to take the strongpoint of Falfemont Farm, to the south-east.

French troops captured Foret.

The Battles of Delville Wood and Pozières both ended with tactical victories for the Allies.

William Allen, a Captain in the RAMC, won his VC at Mesnil on the Somme when, under heavy shellfire, he attended and rescued wounded comrades from the battlefield.

At Guillemont, three other VCs were also awarded to Lieutenant John Holland, Sergeant David Jones and Private Thomas Hughes.

September 4, 1916 – A second British attack on Falfemont Farm failed.

Haig met with Rawlinson; although the taking of Guillemont was a positive sign, he emphasised the importance of pressing on further eastward.

At the same time, French troops continued the offensive, taking Barleux and Chilly and a substantial number of prisoners in the process.

September 5, 1916 – British troops captured parts of Leuze Wood during the Battle of Guillemont, allowing the Allies to occupy the whole of the German second line. During the night Falfemont Farm was taken.

September 1916

September 6, 1916 – The Battle of Guillemont ended with the British consolidating their hold on the village and completing the advance towards Ginchy. The remainder of Leuze Wood was secured.
On a visit to the Front, Asquith inspected the ruins of Fricourt, which had been captured by the British at the start of the Somme Offensive in early July.
New Zealand passed a Bill for compulsory military service.

September 8, 1916 – German troops failed to oust the French at Berny to the south of Chaulnes.
It was reported that Hindenburg visited the Western Front for first time.

September 9, 1916 – In the intermediate phase of the offensive, British troops captured the German-held village of Ginchy, a strategically important post. Trenches were also taken to the north and east of Leuze Wood.
A series of conferences was held in Paris between the British Secretary for War, Lloyd George, the British Minister for Munitions and their French counterparts to discuss recent operations and effective deployment of resources.
South Wales railwaymen voted unanimously to strike the following week unless they were given a 10s-a-week increase in the basic pay.
Canadian Corporal Leo Clarke was posthumously awarded his VC for actions at Pozières.

September 10, 1916 – A German counter-attack at Ginchy was repulsed as British troops continued to advance to the east of Guillemont.

September 12, 1916 – The British bombarded enemy lines in preparation for the attack on 15 September. French troops captured the area to the south of Combles as far as the Somme River. Lloyd George visited Méaulte on the Somme with Albert Thomas, the French Minister of Munitions.

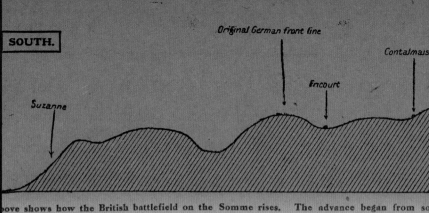

THE RIDGE WH

SOUTH.

Original German front line

Contalmais

Encourt

Suzanne

ove shows how the British battlefield on the Somme rises. The advance began from so
n front line" is marked. The top of the hill north of Pozières has been reached

Opposite below: **Canadians** go over the top, but this time the advance is aided by the appearance of tanks on the battlefield for the first time. This new armoured monster terrified many German soldiers.

Above: **Canadians** escort German prisoners down a communication trench near Courcelette. They were only too eager to cry "Kamerad" to protect themselves.

Opposite above right: Members of a Highland regiment on their way to the trenches.

Top: A graphic published on 15 August showing the terrain of the battlefield and the original front line just south of Fricourt.

CANADIANS ON THE SOMME—THE PUSH OF THE BIG G

PICK-AXES FORWARD.—These sturdy Canadians, carrying pick-axes, are seen going forward to consolidate and organise some of our recent gains of ground on the Somme. [Canadian Official Photograph]

TOWARDS BAPAUME!—A big artillery unit in the colossal struggle on the Somme. Such guns are doing their routine work of smashing the German receding positions, prefatory to the fine advance of the Allies' waves of infantry. [French Official]

"ZEPPELIN STRAFER" AT MACHINE-GUN PRA
Lieutenant Brandon, D.S.O., one of the R.F.C. officers m
for gallantry in the air, trying a machine gun. [Daily

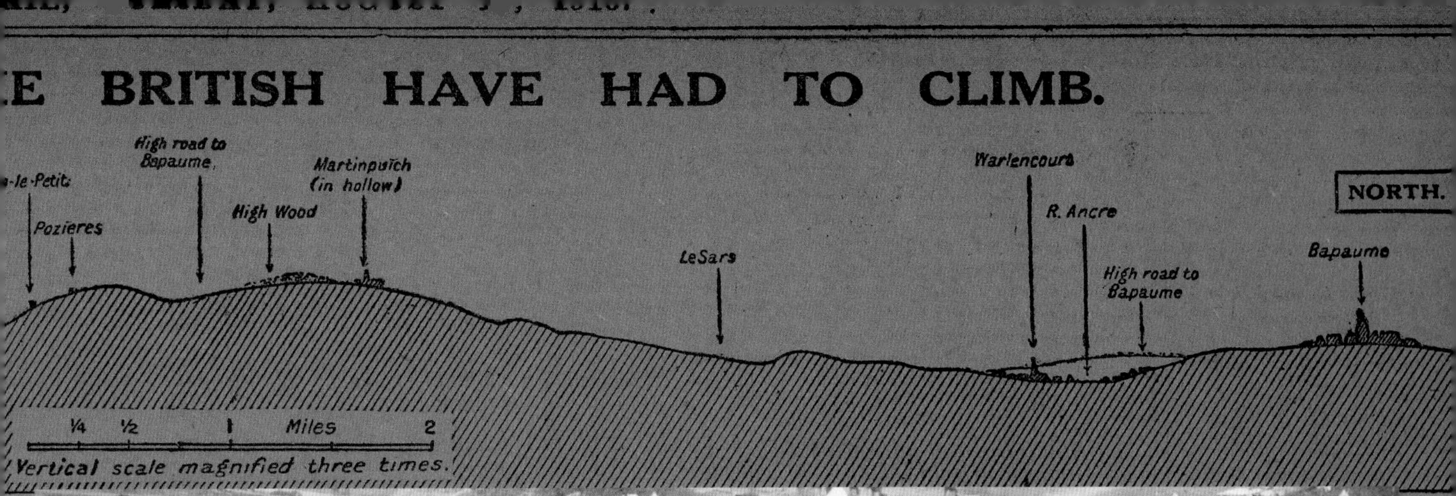
E BRITISH HAVE HAD TO CLIMB.
-le-Petit
Pozieres
High road to Bapaume
High Wood
Martinpuich (in hollow)
LeSars
Warlencourt
R. Ancre
High road to Bapaume
Bapaume
NORTH.
1/4 1/2 1 Miles 2
Vertical scale magnified three times.

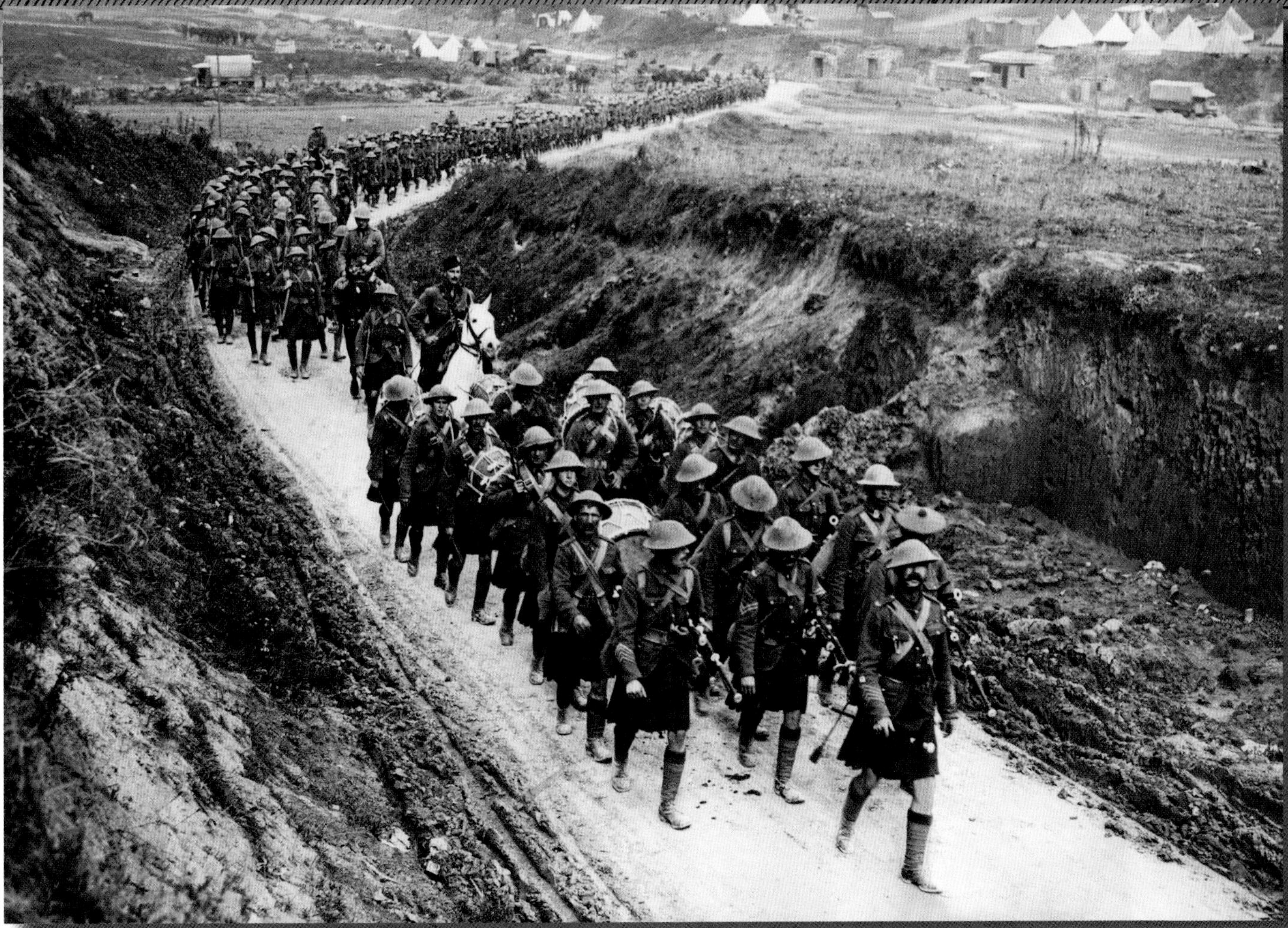

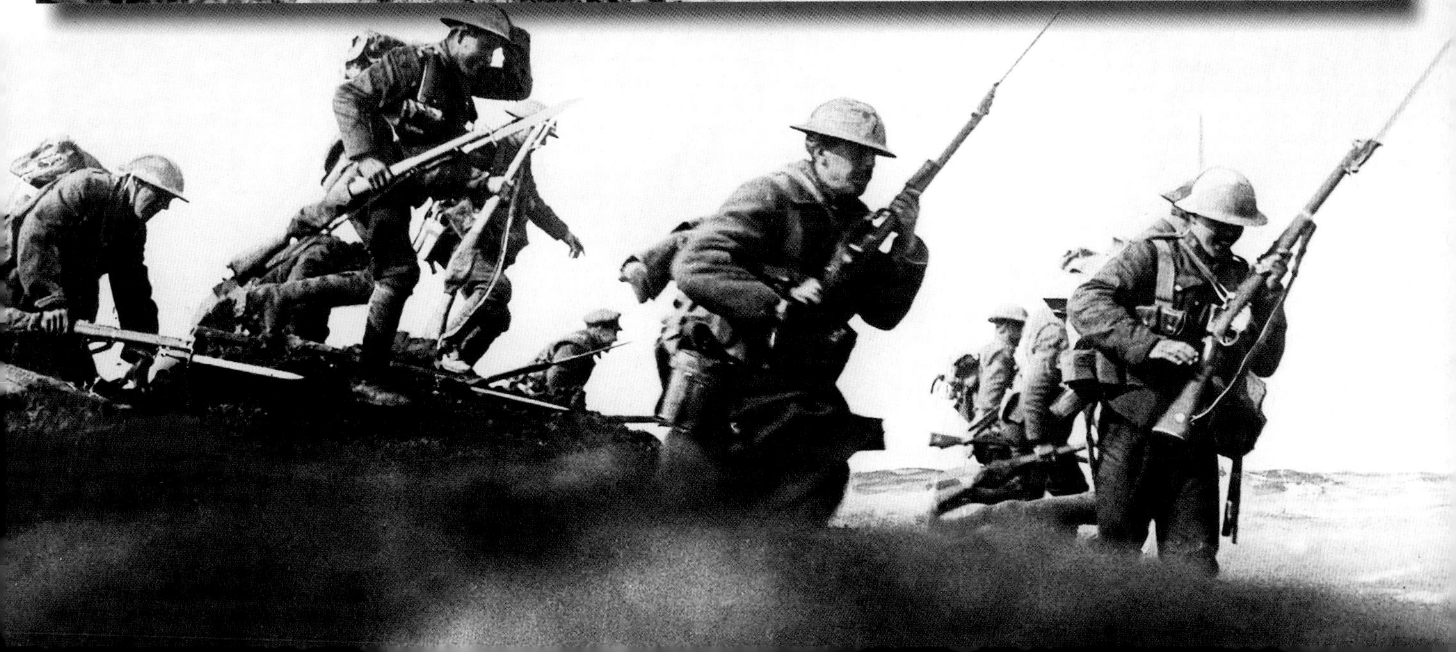

Tanks fail to tilt balance at the Somme

Aside from the fact that the initial artillery bombardment failed to wreak the anticipated devastation on the German positions, from the outset there were strategic fault lines in the Somme offensive. Haig saw it as an opportunity for a major breakthrough, while Rawlinson favoured setting limited objectives and consolidation: a "bite and hold" approach. As the battle wore on, the aim seemed to drift between the two. There were opportunities to penetrate the enemy ranks in a way that would have gladdened Haig's heart, but when they weren't capitalised upon it became politic to present limited gains as delivering attritional body blows to the enemy.

Those brighter moments included an audacious dawn attack on 14 July that caught the Germans off guard. Two months later, the British deployed their new secret weapon, christened from the "water tank" cover name assigned when it was under wraps. The brainchild of one Colonel Ernest Swinton, it was Churchill at the Admiralty who took up cudgels on behalf of this armoured attack vehicle that ran on caterpillar tracks. Exactly one year before the tank first appeared on the battlefield it had been a wooden model. Fifty had been built by the time of the 15 September attack at Flers; fewer than Haig expected, but he was keen to see if they could make a difference in an offensive that was already ten weeks old. They couldn't. Tanks that made it through to confront the enemy did create panic and confusion, but this was infant technology and early models were unreliable, prone to becoming bogged down and not as impervious to shellfire as might have been expected. One tank commander lost his bearings and fired on his own line. It was clearly a military innovation that had much promise, though unleashed, perhaps, too soon. Certainly tanks did not swing the Somme offensive dramatically in the Allies' favour; their day would come the following year.

SIR D. HAIG WINS AT SMALL COST.

THE DASH OF THE TANKS.

HUN CRY: 'UNFAIR BUTCHERY.'

TWO BRITISH BATTALIONS BEAT A BRIGADE IN THE OPEN.

MR. BEACH THOMAS'S BRILLIANT DESPATCH.

It was clearly a military innovation that had much promise, though unleashed, perhaps, too soon.

IS AT | verted into a fortress, guarded them on their left, a machine-gun redoubt on their right, wire and barricades | THE KING TO SIR DOUGLAS HAIG | self was not attacked till after six in the evening; and was not in our hands till 7.30 | fortified position arrested our adva Farther south again we advanced point near the end of Beulah Wood a

Above right: French tanks take part in an organised attack on German lines. The French had been developing their own tank models at the same time as the British, but whereas Britain had opted to join all its expertise together to produce the Mark I, several independent companies had designed and made the French models.

Opposite bottom: Tanks were manned by three drivers, a subaltern and four gunners, including an NCO. The noise, exhaust fumes and heat were intense and crew members were often sick or unwell even after very short journeys.

Below: The C24 was a "female" tank going by the name of Clan Cameron. Its commander was Captain Harold Cole who was awarded the MBE after the war.

Opposite top and above left: The first official photographs of tanks going into action at the Battle of Flers-Courcelette were released after the new weapon was taken off the secrets list. The British Mark I "male" tank carried two Hotchkiss 6-pounder guns and four machine-guns. It had a tail wheel designed to provide balance, but after proving to be ineffective this was abandoned in later models.

E BRITISH CAPTURE OF FLERS.—In a despatch dated September 19 a correspondent states that the men who took Flers were mainly from the London area. The photograph shows some forcements moving towards the village from a German trench taken on September 15. These men doubtless saw what "The Times" correspondent calls "one of the finest sights of a thrilling day," the spectacle of one huge tank in the main street of Flers all alone while Hun rifles and machine guns played on it like harmless pea-shooters. [Official Photograph.]

HE DAILY MAIL,

BRITISH AIRMEN DRO

Y OF AIR RAIDS BEHIND

GERMAN LINES.

LATE WAR

ZEPPELIN

MO

CRUISE

War in the air

Aeronautical technology moved on apace during the 1914-18 period, and with it the role of aircraft as an instrument of war altered radically. Compared with the giant, gas-filled airships with their large payloads, most of the heavier-than-air machines in service at the outbreak of hostilities were puny indeed. Typically around 25-feet long, with fabric stretched over wooden frames, these early aircraft were powered by small rotary or in-line engines that might propel a two-man crew through the air at 70mph. Nor were there many of them. The Royal Flying Corps, established in 1912 as the air-arm of the British Army, had fewer than 50 machines at its disposal when the events in Sarajevo sparked the global conflict.

Barely a decade on from the Wright brothers' breakthrough, the main military application of these flimsy, rudimentary craft was thought to be reconnaissance and observation – the new sky-riding cavalry scouts – and indeed that was their chief role throughout the early days of the Great War. But the pre-war opinion of French general Ferdinand Foch that aviation was fine as a sporting pursuit but offered nothing to the battlefield was being disproved, as firepower was added and RFC planes moved into the more active role of aerial combat with German pilots: there was a clear advantage in gathering intelligence on enemy positions while preventing rival aircraft from doing likewise. Trench-strafing and, later in the war, the strategic bombing of German cities and factories followed.

By late 1915, Germany had established air superiority with the development of gear-synchronisation, allowing machine-guns to fire through the blades of the propellers. This advantage had changed in the Allies' favour by the following spring as both Britain and France established specialist fighter squadrons.

The strength of the Royal Flying Corps in the Somme area was 185 aircraft against the German 2nd Army aircraft establishment, which also had to face the Aviation Militaire on the south bank of the Somme. Reconnaissance on 1 July allowed RFC pilots to advise the ground commanders on the effects of the previous week's bombardment. Bombing attacks were to be made on the railways behind the German front to ensure that damage could not be repaired in the days after the beginning of the offensive. Troops, transport columns, dumps and headquarters behind the battlefront were to be attacked and the ammunition depots at Mons, Namur and Lille.

In the last weeks of the Somme Offensive Germany reorganised its Air Corps to form the *Luftstreitkrafte*, which included the specialist fighter squadrons of the *Jagdstaffein*. By April 1918, the Royal Flying Corps had merged with the Royal Naval Air Service to form the RAF.

IS

THE MURDER OF CAPT. FRYATT.

MR. ASQUITH'S PROMISE.

MAKE THEM PAY.

THE WIDOW'S PENSION

RUSSIAN ADVANCE ON KOVEL.

GERMANS PREPARING STRONG DEFENCE

NEW IRISH PLAN.

MR. DUKE AS RESIDENT CHIEF SECRETARY.

AND

Opposite: This Lewis anti-aircraft gun is fixed on a cartwheel that revolves on its axis set into a socket on the ground. These guns were often used in defence against aircraft as they were light, air-cooled and had their own 97-round drum magazines.

Below: A German plane is photographed minutes after French airmen force it to the ground.

Right: A French pilot uses a machine gun during a nosedive.

Top: Newspaper headline, August 1, 1916, one month into the Somme campaign.

LATE WAR NEWS.

EVERY MAN UNDER 41 CALLED UP.

◆

TO REPORT BY JULY 24.

HOME WORK PREFERENCE TO LAST GROUPS.

All the married conscripts are called up by one proclamation issued to-day. They are deemed soldiers on **June 24**. The proclamation states that unless a notice is received to join up beforehand, married conscripts must report on **July 24**.

This means that on July 24 every man of military age up to forty-one—married or single—will be in the Army—or Navy—unless specially exempted, rejected as unfit, or passed on to war work.

LAST APPEAL DAY.

A War Office statement, issued at 12.40 this morning, stated that an application by or in respect of a man under the Compulsion Act must be made to a local tribunal *before June* 24 if it is desired to secure his exemption.

Badge men, if in any doubt as to their position, should inquire of the local recruiting officer, producing certificate for inspection.

Groups close *next Wednesday,* except to men formerly rejected on medical grounds and lads.

An application for exemption by or in respect of a man who now voluntarily attests must be handed in within ten days of attesting.

DERBY MEN'S ADVANTAGE.

The last groups of attested married men are under orders to begin to report themselves on June 13. But a War Office announcement yesterday gives them an important preference over the conscripts by calling for the first instalment of men for war work at home. One thousand are wanted now, and only attested men in Groups 42 to 46 (ages thirty-six to forty) will be accepted. They will not be taken for service in the field so long as they are employed on this special w␣k and will not be under military control. Pay, from 8¼d. to 9¼d. per hour (£1 14s. to £ 18s. a week of forty-eight hours).

Full information can be obtained at the Inquiry Office, Great Scotland Yard.

A representative of *The Daily Mail* was informed at the War Office yesterday that the offer marks the beginning of a policy under which it is hoped to retain in civil life most, if not all, of the attested married men aged 36 to 40 by employing them in war work at home.

Conscription increased in advance of the "Big Push"

Until January 1916 Britain shunned coercion as a means of prosecuting the war. For 17 months, Regulars, Territorials and Reservists, augmented by Kitchener's volunteers, made up Britain's fighting force. Every effort was made to put persuasion before compulsion. Within weeks of the War Secretary's famous recruitment drive, the age limit was raised to 35, and the response was such that the machinery by which men were adopted into uniform struggled to cope. In spring 1915 the pinch-point was munitions, not men, regardless of the fact that the BEF had been all but wiped out. But as the "shell scandal" was addressed the military manpower issue became a growing concern. In February 1915 the monthly enlistment figure dropped to under 100,000 for the first time, a decline replicated throughout the year.

On 27 January 1916 the Military Service Act brought single men aged 18-41 into the conscription net, Britain joining the other major belligerents in making soldiering a matter of statutory obligation.

There were 750,000 exemption applications in the first six months following the passing of the Military Service Act. Tribunals were set up to hear such cases and became increasingly stringent over time.

Single men were drafted into the army alongside the first conscript wave in spring 1916. Still the figures disappointed, and in early May the first of the married volunteers were summoned to the Colours. A month later saw the Military Service Act amended to make all married men up to the age of 41 liable to the call-up. Thus numbers swelled in time for the planned advance at the Somme.

Below: In May 1916 a second Military Service Act was passed, extending conscription to married men. The first groups who responded to the call are pictured marching down Whitehall.

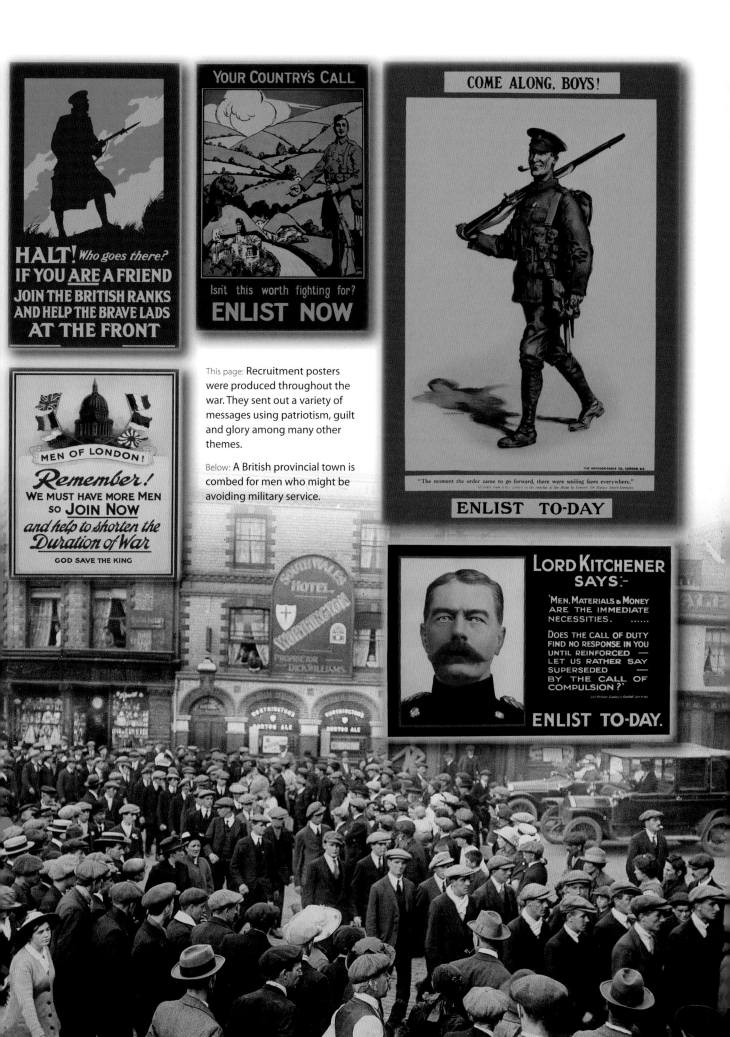

HALT! *Who goes there?*
IF YOU ARE A FRIEND
JOIN THE BRITISH RANKS
AND HELP THE BRAVE LADS
AT THE FRONT

YOUR COUNTRY'S CALL
Isn't this worth fighting for?
ENLIST NOW

COME ALONG, BOYS!

"The moment the order came to go forward, there were smiling faces everywhere."
Illustrate from letter written in the trenches of the Aisne by General Sir Horace Smith-Dorrien.

ENLIST TO-DAY

MEN OF LONDON!
Remember!
WE MUST HAVE MORE MEN
SO **JOIN NOW**
and help to shorten the
Duration of War
GOD SAVE THE KING

This page: Recruitment posters were produced throughout the war. They sent out a variety of messages using patriotism, guilt and glory among many other themes.

Below: A British provincial town is combed for men who might be avoiding military service.

LORD KITCHENER SAYS:
'MEN, MATERIALS & MONEY ARE THE IMMEDIATE NECESSITIES. ......
DOES THE CALL OF DUTY FIND NO RESPONSE IN YOU UNTIL REINFORCED — LET US RATHER SAY SUPERSEDED — BY THE CALL OF COMPULSION?'
Lord Kitchener, Guildhall Speech, July 9 1915

ENLIST TO-DAY.

Large scale map of the battle ground described in Mr. Beach Thomas's message. The dotted section in the map indicates approximately the ground gained by the British between Thiepval and Combles since Friday morning.

TANK MOVING INTO ACTION

INFANTRY MOVING FORWARD

INFANTRY WAITING TO ADVANCE

HOW THE TANKS GO INTO BATTLE.—A scene in Tank and trench operations on the Western Front. [Official]

Above: Motor lorries filled with Allied troops pass through a Somme village. The British Army began the war with just over 500 vehicles and by the end possessed 22,000 trucks.

Below: New Zealanders carry their kit as they move up to the trenches. The country had already introduced partial military conscription in 1909 and had been the first Dominion to send troops to assist the Allies. A total of 120,000 men saw active service during the conflict.

Opposite: Infantrymen wait in the safety of the trenches as a tank (top left) moves in on the attack.

BRITISH ADVANC

M TWO LINES
ENCHES.

CREEPING UP TO COMBLES.

THE

FRENCH STORM HOUSE FORT.

A WIDE FRONT

*Driving forward behind a creeping barrage,
the infantry enjoyed a resounding success.*

ON A MILE FRONT.

LE TRUTH FROM ATHENS.

ONSTANTINE'S POSITION.

From J. M. N. JEFFRIES

OUR AIRMEN FIGH INFANTRY.

BOMBERS' EXPLOITS

Battle of Morval

Below: Reserves move up to support the advance on Morval. Poor weather had caused the attack to be postponed by a few days and the heavy rain and fog grounded aircraft and affected artillery observation, while infantrymen floundered in the mud.

On 25 September, three days after Flers-Courcelette, the Allies renewed their attack, a north-easterly push by Rawlinson's 4th Army, with the French 6th Army to its right. Morval had been one of the immediate targets of the assault launched on 15 September, and it was even more firmly in Haig's sights ten days later. The idea was to push through reinforcements – including cavalry – and establish a flank guard along a line connecting Morval with Bapaume; forces that would assail the enemy from the side and rear while the frontal attack continued.

By the time the Battle of Morval opened, the objectives were more modest, the kind of "bite-and-hold" operation favoured by Rawlinson. In particular, the advance would remain within the compass of covering artillery, which was concentrated on a narrower front and correspondingly more effective. It was a daylight advance, launched just after noon, British commanders yielding to their French counterparts' preference regarding the timing. The available tanks this time were held back, since concealment ahead of the battle would have been impossible and the surprise element lost. That freed the gunners from having to leave lanes clear to accommodate them.

Driving forward behind an effective creeping barrage, the infantry in some cases reached the enemy line before the defenders were fully prepared. They enjoyed a resounding success, quickly taking possession of Lesboeufs – another missed target from ten days earlier – as well as Morval itself. The Germans yielded Combles to the French the following day, at the end of which Gueudecourt was also in Allied hands.

It was an impressive 48 hours' work, and Haig was buoyed by such progress at relatively little cost. On 27 September, he recorded: "Total casualties for the last two days are just 8,000. This is very remarkable, and seems to bear out the idea that the Enemy is not fighting so well, and has suffered in moral (sic)." The latter observation, history shows, was over-optimistic, but the Battle of Morval was undoubtedly a solid success for the Allies. However, the cautious, measured approach also provided the Germans with breathing space in which to regroup and form a fresh defensive line.

September 1916

September 14, 1916 – German trenches to the south-east of Thiepval were stormed by British troops who captured the Wunderwerk Redoubt (the Wonderwork). As Haig visited Rawlinson urging that the attack the following day on Martinpuich should be intense, British troops moved up in preparation for the start of the major new offensive.

September 15, 1916 – The Battle of Flers-Courcelette began and saw the first deployment of British armoured tanks when the British Fourth Army launched this large-scale offensive. The battle signified the start of the third stage of the Somme offensive, and was a day of significant progress for the British: Flers, Martinpuich, Courcelette and High Wood were all taken.
French troops moved to the south of Rancourt and captured a system of enemy trenches north of Le Priez Farm.
Herbert Asquith's son Raymond was killed during the battle as he led some of his Company in an attack near Ginchy. Sergeant Donald Brown, Lieutenant Colonel John Campbell and Lance Sergeant Fred McNess were each awarded the VC for their part on the opening day of the Battle of Flers-Courcelette.

September 16, 1916 – Despite a German counter-attack at Courcelette, the British continued to advance, taking Danube Trench and Mouquet Farm.
New Zealand troops progressed north and west of Flers. Private John Kerr of the Canadian Expeditionary Force received the VC for his brave actions at Courcelette.

September 18, 1916 – South of the Ancre River, a northern tributary of the Somme, the British Sixth Division took the fortified German position known as the Quadrilateral between Ginchy and Bouleux Wood to a depth of a thousand yards.
French troops captured the village of Deniécourt in the south.

September 20, 1916 – As bad weather hindered the moving up of armaments, the Commander of the British Fourth Army, General Henry Rawlinson, delayed the next attack on the German frontline until 23 September. A German counter-attack at Combles failed.
On the Eastern Front, the Brusilov Offensive stalled. A major Russian attack against the armies of the Central Powers designed to draw German units away from the Somme and Verdun, it was largely successful in its objective but by September Russian casualties were considerable, reaching almost a million men. Low morale and an undignified withdrawal of the troops led to social and political unrest in Russia.

Below: Once the signal is given, troops leave their trenches at Morval. A shell can be seen exploding in the distance.

Fremicourt

Velu

R. E.

BAPAUME

MONDAY, OCTOBER 2, 1916.

Price 6d. Post free 7d.
From Map Publisher, Carmelite House, E.C.

PICTORIAL MAP OF THE SOMME FRONT

La Barque

Villers

Barastre

Beaulencourt

The white arrows show approximately the British and French fronts between the Ancre and the Somme as indicated by official reports at the beginning of October 1916.

Gueudecourt

Flers

le Transloy

Rocquigny

Lebœufs

le Mesnil

Morval

Longueval

Ginchy

Sailly

Etri

Manan

Guillemont

Combles

LeForest

Rancourt

R. TORTILLE

Maurepas

Moislains

Bouch-avesnes

Allaines

Aizec le H

Cléry

Curlu

Hem

Mt St Quentin

Drier

Frise

R. SOMM

Battle of Thiepval

Twenty-four hours after the attack on Morval was launched, Allied attention turned to the northern side of the Albert-Bapaume road, the left flank of the "Big Push". On 26 September General Gough's Reserve Army faced its greatest challenge to date as it began its assault on Thiepval. This village, on a spur overlooking the Ancre valley, had been pounded since the opening day, when it was meant to have fallen. Thus far it had proved resilient. While the buildings were heavily battle scarred, there were plenty of cellars that German machine-gunners put to good use.

Four divisions, two of them Canadian, attacked on a 6,000-yard front, which extended eastwards to Courcelette. As well as the village itself, the targets also included three redoubts. Tanks were again deployed, and though only a handful were available they were used to good effect as German strongpoints in Thiepval itself offered dogged resistance.

Day One was by no means uniformly successful, though 18th Division, under the inspired leadership of Major General Ivor Maxse, made it to Zollern trench, a launchpad for the capture of the village itself. Thiepval was cleared by the morning of the 27th, and Gough's men also established a significant foothold on the ridge running from Thiepval to Courcelette. The two remaining redoubts, Schwaben and Stuff, witnessed much close-quarter fighting and proved more difficult to gain command of than Zollern. The defensive forces dug in there would not be fully dislodged until the next phase of the battle. Even so, the balance sheet for the second half of September made encouraging reading: gains made over that fortnight were comparable to the aggregate for the first two-and-a-half months of the Somme offensive.

Left: German prisoners are led out from a trench in Thiepval. The village was taken by the Allies on 27 September.

Below: British soldiers watch for the enemy. Thiepval marked the first major battle for the Reserve Army under the command of Lieutenant-General Sir Hubert Gough.

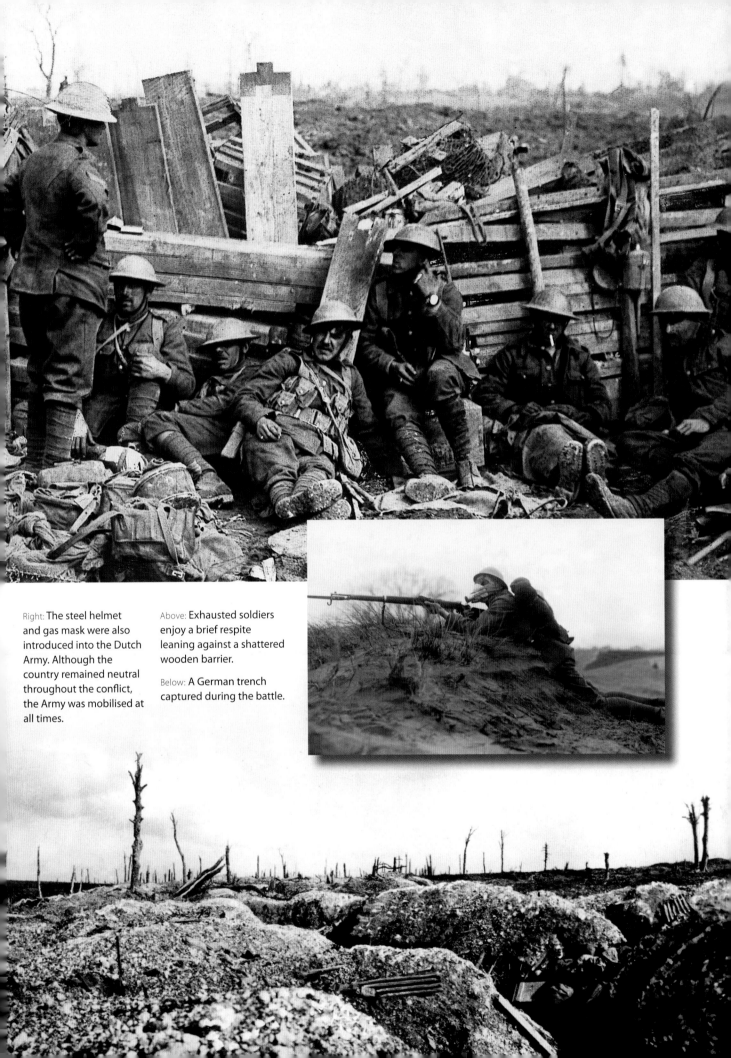

Right: The steel helmet and gas mask were also introduced into the Dutch Army. Although the country remained neutral throughout the conflict, the Army was mobilised at all times.

Above: Exhausted soldiers enjoy a brief respite leaning against a shattered wooden barrier.

Below: A German trench captured during the battle.

September 1916

September 21, 1916 – British troops moved forward between Flers and Martinpuich, south of the Ancre.

September 22, 1916 – The Battle of Flers-Courcelette ended; the strategic objective of a breakthrough had not been achieved although tactical gains had been made with the capture of the villages Martinpuich, Courcelette and Flers.

September 23, 1916 – Twelve Zeppelins bombed London and the English east coast. Two of the invading aircraft were brought down.
The operations to take Morval, delayed until 23 September, were again postponed for a further two days.

September 24, 1916 – French aircraft bombed the Krupp munitions works at Essen in Germany.
The German airmen who survived a Zeppelin crash in the Essex countryside were arrested by the village constable.

September 25, 1916 – The Battle of Morval began with an attack by the British Fourth Army on the German-held villages of Morval, Gueudecourt and Lesbœufs with another successful use of tanks.
French troops moved forward at Rancourt, Le Priez Farm and Frégicourt.
Private Thomas Jones was awarded his VC for his actions in an advance on the first day of the Battle of Morval.

September 26, 1916 – The Battle of Thiepval Ridge began with the aim of building on the Fourth Army attack the previous day.
Allied troops attacked and captured the villages of Thiepval and Combles.
Private Frederick Edwards and Private Robert Ryder, both of the Middlesex Regiment, received their VCs for their actions at Thiepval.

September 27, 1916 – British troops took Stuff Redoubt and advanced to the north of Flers.
Both Second Lieutenant Tom Adlam and Captain Archie White were fighting at Thiepval when they were awarded their VCs. Adlam led an attack on part of the village despite being wounded in the leg. Captain White, over a period of four days and nights, held Stuff Redoubt under heavy German fire and several counter-attacks.

September 28, 1916 – As the British attacked and captured most of the Schwaben Redoubt on the crest of the Thiepval Plateau, the Battles of Morval and Thiepval Ridge ended in victory for the Allied forces.

September 29, 1916 – "Meatless" days were suggested in Britain as food shortages begin to bite and prices to rise.
Germany criticised the US and called into question its neutrality by allowing Americans to join the Allied air forces.

Above: The Canadian Infantry march to the front line in October, 1916. Over 600,000 Canadians took part in the war with 170,000 wounded and 60,000 losing their lives. To recognise the significant part they played, the country was accorded its own representative at the Paris Peace Conference and signed the treaties as a separate nation, although it remained part of the British Empire.

Battle of Transloy Ridge

Allied successes in the second half of September left Haig in upbeat mood, determined to build on the gains already made as the Somme offensive entered its fourth month. He envisaged driving through Bapaume and even reaching Cambrai a further 15 miles to the northeast. Standing in his way was the new German front line, which ran along the ridge at Le Transloy, four miles south of Bapaume. Further trenches were being constructed beyond, giving a formidably deep defence mirroring that which the Allies faced on 1 July. Allied reconnaissance confirmed that these new fortifications were rapidly being established. That news, in turn, stiffened the resolve of the German frontline troops. There was comfort to be had in knowing there was a formidable defensive system to the rear, defences strengthening by the hour. Among those arriving at the front to help counter the next Allied onslaught was the regiment of Corporal Adolf Hitler.

Undeterred, Haig drew up his ambitious plan, which had Rawlinson's 4th Army attacking Le Transloy Ridge, with General Allenby's 3rd Army driving towards the high ground near Gommecourt in the north. Allenby's forces would offer flank protection to Gough's Reserve Army as they pushed eastward. On the right of the attacking front the French 6th and 10th Armies were pressed into action. Rawlinson thought it a bold enterprise with much to recommend it, but as if there were not enough uncertainties on the battlefield, October brought another: the gloomy prospect of deteriorating weather.

This first phase, undertaken by Rawlinson's 4th Army, commenced on 1 October. The capture of Le Sars a week later proved something of a false dawn. Haig had judged that the picture would be brighter once Le Sars, which straddled the Albert-Bapaume road, was taken, since the topography would then make the effective deployment of artillery considerably easier. Things did not pan out that way. Resistance was ferocious, casualties heavy, gains strictly limited. Poor visibility hampered aerial support, and at ground level it was difficult to pinpoint German positions with accuracy. And the terrain was rapidly becoming a glutinous quagmire, making the movement of supplies and equipment extraordinarily burdensome.

Haig was in a cleft stick. The situation might have called for discretion, but he was determined not to provide the enemy with the latitude that might allow him to recover and strengthen. As October wore on the attacks became piecemeal, and the battle ended after a failed assault on 5 November, in which Rawlinson had little faith but which Haig insisted go ahead.

The frustrations of the Transloy operation left Haig's resolve undented, his grand design intact. As it was fizzling towards a suspension of hostilities, he wrote: "...the war was only to be won by defeating the Germans. This could not be done in the Balkans but only in France. So all possible means should be sent to France, and the Enemy should be pressed continuously – right through the winter whenever the weather permitted."

Above and opposite top: A light-hearted moment as soldiers optimistically suggest that the wreckage of a Hansom cab might make it to the seat of government.

Opposite: Two Canadian official kinema operators film a battle on the horizon. On the right a photographer is at work, while two artillery observers are busy alongside them. At the start of the war Lord Kitchener banned British journalists from directly reporting on hostilities and instead appointed Colonel Ernest Swinton to write reports that were vetted by Kitchener before being sent to the newspapers.

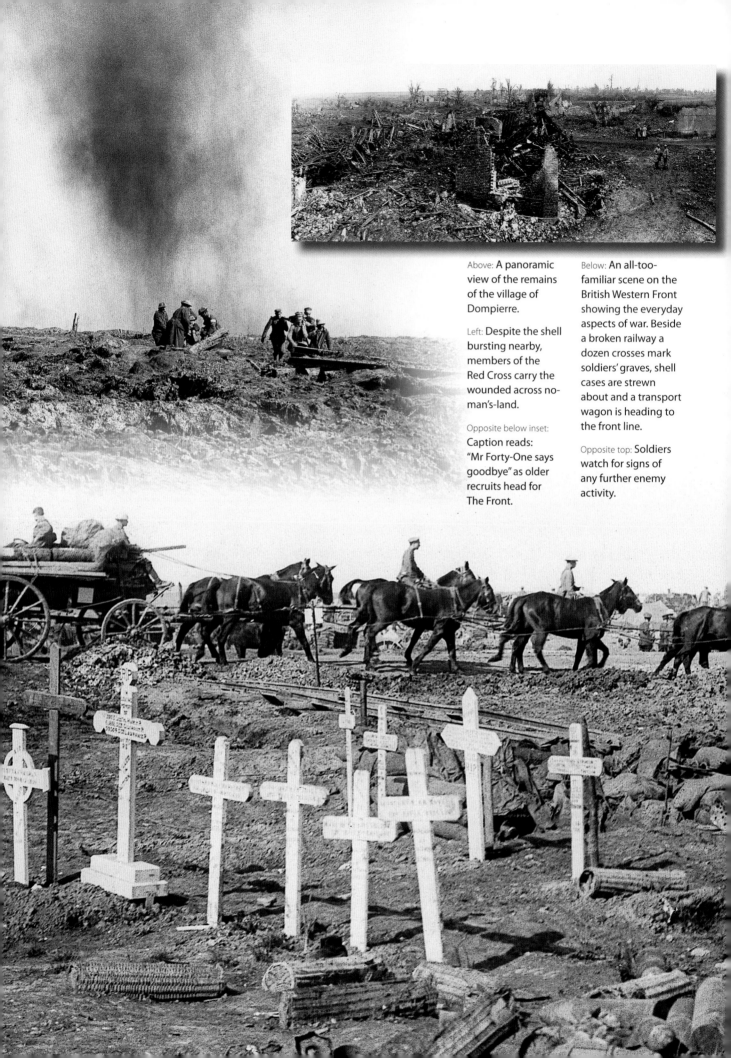

Above: **A panoramic view of the remains of the village of Dompierre.**

Left: **Despite the shell bursting nearby, members of the Red Cross carry the wounded across no-man's-land.**

Opposite below inset: **Caption reads: "Mr Forty-One says goodbye" as older recruits head for The Front.**

Below: **An all-too-familiar scene on the British Western Front showing the everyday aspects of war. Beside a broken railway a dozen crosses mark soldiers' graves, shell cases are strewn about and a transport wagon is heading to the front line.**

Opposite top: **Soldiers watch for signs of any further enemy activity.**

The capture of Le Sars on 7 October was something of a false dawn. Resistance was ferocious.

October 1916

October 1, 1916 – As a preliminary to Haig's longer term autumn offensive, the Battle of the Ancre Heights began with attacks on the redoubts of Stuff and Schwaben.

The Battle of the Transloy Ridges, part of the Ancre Heights offensive, also began as British troops attacked towards Eaucourt-Le Sars and Eaucourt L'Abbaye.

Eleven Zeppelins make a raid on Britain's east coast and London.

Lieutenant Colonel Roland Boys Bradford was awarded his VC for his brave actions and cool leadership in the attack on Eaucourt L'Abbaye.

October 2, 1916 – Heavy rain deluged the whole of the Somme front as the Allies moved forward.

October 3, 1916 – Eaucourt L'Abbaye was secured by the British.

October 4, 1916 – Further rain delayed progress although French troops were able to take the enemy line between Morval and St. Pierre Vaast Wood.

Second Lieutenant Henry Kelly received his VC for his actions at the Battle of Le Transloy.

October 5, 1916 – American President Woodrow Wilson said the US was prepared to fight a "just cause".

British troops advanced north-east of Eaucourt as the French progressed east of Morval.

Heavy rain continued to fall, turning the whole of the Somme front to a muddy swamp which made more difficult the movement of troops and supplies.

October 7, 1916 – Despite the bad weather, the Allies made advances along the Albert-Bapaume Road, capturing Le Sars.

October 8, 1916 –As the British line continued to advance beyond Courcelette, German troops resisted repeated attacks on the Schwaben Redoubt.

Germany's aerial fighting groups merged to form the Luftstreikrafte, which included its fighter wing, the Jasta squadrons.

During an attack on the German front line at Regina Trench, Private James Richardson galvanised his comrades into action by playing his pipes in full view of the enemy, for which he was posthumously awarded the VC.

8 Cards in a Set 6d. ON SALE EVERYWHERE

SATURDAY, NOVEMBER 11, 1916.

Cut the picture you want from a newspaper and send with remittance to War Picture Dept., "Daily Mail," Carmelite House, E.C.

SAMPLES OF SOMME MUD IN OFFICIAL PICTURES.

A MORNING STROLL IN PICARDY.—"Squish—squish—slip—slosh!" Just an ordinary kind of experience when one passes along a road behind the British lines these days. [Official Photograph.

THE WET ROAD FROM THE TRENCHES.—The infantryman suffers most from mud and water, the roads becoming at once "incredibly slippery and impossibly tenacious." This picture shows a Middlesex battalion returning on such a road to their quarters, several wounded men being wheeled by their comrades. [Official Photograph.

MUD-TIRED WORCESTERS.—"Each dragging footstep calls for a tremendous effort." That is why these Worcesters have stepped out of the mud to take delicious rest on a mud bank! [Official Photograph.

A BOG IN THE BALKANS.—Not only in the Somme regions, but in the Balkans too, the floods are out, and this picture shows a wandering waste of water and mud through which a motor-car is being tugged by a team of six Serbian artillery horses. [Official.

"MUD TERRACE, W."—If, wrote a soldier, in "The Daily Mail," "a man would know why we do not advance . . . let him walk on a dark night through the village duck-pond, and then sleep in his wet clothes in the middle of the farmyard." [Official Photograph.

Battle of Ancre

As the Somme offensive rolled into November, Haig wanted one last flourish ahead of the mid-month Allied conference at Chantilly; a fresh prize he could trumpet before the weather rendered further action impossible. It would be both fillip and spur to the Allies if he could attend the meeting "on top of the capture of Beaumont Hamel for instance, and 3,000 German prisoners". As for the War Committee, now openly expressing reservations about the achievements thus far and the wisdom of continuing, any good news would be welcome. They – and Lloyd George in particular – were beginning to question whether attacking on a different front might bring greater benefit for less cost.

Germany was not broken, but the four-and-a-half-month offensive had "placed beyond doubt" the ability of the Allies to prevail in the great struggle.

Gough's 5th Army – the reconstituted Reserve Army – was tasked with delivering the bounty, and to that end attacked astride the Ancre on 13 November, the date deferred due to adverse conditions. The fact that there had been little movement on this stretch of front was advantageous, for there were not the logistics problems that bedevilled other parts of the line. Movement here was certainly easier. The weather, too, was advantageous for once, mist shrouding the area providing cover from enemy observers. It was a mixed blessing, though, since the attackers bypassed some German gunners, who were able to do their deadly work from the rear.

The battle was in full cry when Haig went to Chantilly, and already there were gains that met his aspirations. By the time the operation wound down on 19 November, 51st (Highland) Division had taken Beaumont Hamel, while 63rd (Royal Naval) Division had control of Beaucourt, which lay on the banks of the Ancre. St Pierre Divion was also in Allied hands. A fourth target, Serre, had not been secured. What sounded like an impressive strike rate had to be set in the context of the original plan, which had all four villages as day-one objectives. Bapaume itself was another of the immediate July targets still in enemy hands when the offensive was closed down. Moreover, those late victories, if a boost to Allied morale, had by no means broken German spirit or brought about an exploitable breach in the enemy's defence.

The end-of-term report contained facts that would be interpreted very differently, both at the time and down the years. The Allies had advanced around six miles at the deepest point of penetration. Casualties amounted to 620,000, British forces accounting for two-thirds of that total. German losses were broadly comparable. A one-for-one attrition rate made better reading for Haig than Ludendorff, since the recruitment pool from the imperial outposts was larger, and the introduction of conscription at home meant there was no immediate manpower concern. Germany had no such luxury, and as we have seen, had already laid plans to withdraw to the the Siegfriedstellung – or Hindenburg Line to the Allies. That shortening of the front, with the consequent savings it brought, would deliver to the Allies gratis far more territory than had been won during the Somme battle at such enormous cost.

Haig, of course, was unaware of how the enemy planned to rationalise its resources over the winter of 1916-17. He struck a positive note: Germany was not broken, but the protracted offensive had "placed beyond doubt" the ability of the Allies to prevail in the great struggle. He also reiterated that the western theatre was key, and that forces deployed elsewhere should be kept to the minimum in order to maximise strength in the main battleground.

Detractors overlook the fact that the construction of the new line was initially a precautionary measure, and that without German losses incurred throughout those four-and-a-half-months, coming hard on the heels of the Verdun casualty count, the enemy would have stood its ground. In other words, the Somme, for all its appalling human cost, forced Germany's hand on the issue of retirement to a more manageable position in the early weeks of 1917.

Opposite: **Injured men from the Middlesex Regiment are wheeled to makeshift hospitals to receive treatment.**

Below: **A Belgian trench mortar gunner waits for the signal to fire.**

Above: **The village of Bucquoy, destroyed in the Battle of Ancre, lies in ruins.**

Opposite above: **A morning stroll in Picardy along a road covered in thick, soup-like mud. By November the weather had further deteriorated but Haig was intent on one more attack before the end of the year.**

Opposite below: **Shell holes soon become useful observation posts.**

Below: **British troops receive dinner rations from field kitchens in the Ancre area.**

"Sham" peace proposal

As general disaffection grew, and the strain of the conflict became more and more apparent, the desire for an end to the war naturally gathered momentum. Germany actually sued for peace on 12 December 1916, but the note that was passed to the Allies was somewhat unusually worded, given its aim. It spoke of the "indestructible strength" of the Central Powers and stated that "a continuation of the war cannot break their resisting power". Perhaps not surprisingly, such language did not have the intended effect; not even the most generous of the Entente Powers could see this as being in any way conciliatory. Lloyd George, who had replaced Asquith as Britain's Prime Minister in December 1916, responded accordingly. It was a "sham proposal", he said, and entering into discussions on the basis of its contents "would be putting our heads in the noose with the rope end in the hands of the Germans". Though all sides may have been eager to end hostilities, they were not willing to do so at any price.

Left: Canadians back from the trenches are given coffee at the canteen.

Below: The front line north and south of Ancre, 15 November, showing the recent gains that include the fortress village of Beaumont-Hamel.

Opposite below: Troops walk alongside the River Ancre. The battle marked the end of the Somme offensive during which six miles were gained along a 16-mile front.

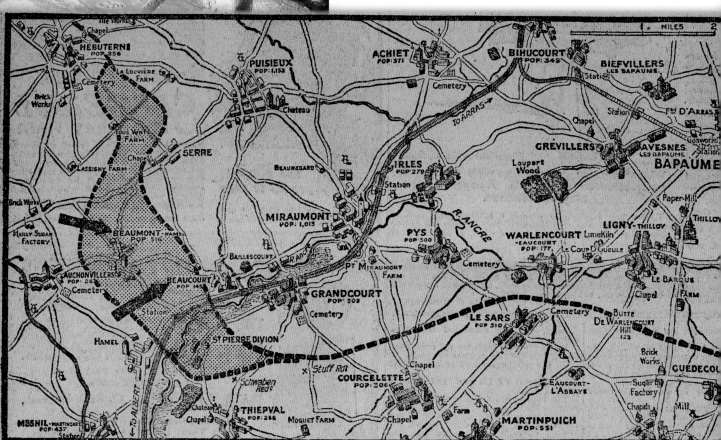

WHERE SIR DOUGLAS HAIG IS PUSHING THEM BACK.—New British front north and south of the Ancre. The extent of our new gains as indicated in the early reports yesterday is shown in the tinted portion of the map. The gains include the strong fortress village of Beaumont-Hamel which the German was impregnable. "The Daily Mail" Giant Map No. 2 covers this front. Price 6d., from all newsagents and stationers, or 7d. post free from Map Publ. Carmelite House, E.C.

THURSDAY, NOVEMBER 16, 1916.

R DOUGLAS HAIG'S GREAT VICTORY—NEW OFFICIAL PICTURES.

FACE.—Our men in this new
rmed wonders. "Tommy" rests
back from the trenches. [Official.

THE CUP THAT CHEERS.—These are the men who are making us re-draw our maps of the Somme and Ancre regions, and of whom Mr. W. Beach
Thomas writes : "The dash of the infantry to-day, as four months ago, aroused the admiration of all officers." They fought with "almost ludicrous
calmness," and their tea-time mood is expressed in the remark of the man who said "We should have eaten 'em up, if we could have seen 'em properly."
[Official Photograph.

"MOVING IN."—"Tommy" finds a new trenc
fresh and stimulating as we find a new house at h
These troops are the first occupiers. [Offi

BRITISH AND FRENC

SEIZED BY BRITISH.

ADVANCE ON FRONT OF 4½ MILES.

OF SAILLISEL TAKEN.

RRE WOOD ENTERED AND 522 PRISONERS.

AR : 95th DAY.

rain yesterday

REICHSTAG SHUT DOWN.

LEVY EN MASSE STEPS.

NO DISCUSSION.

From CHARLES TOWER.

AMSTERDAM, Sunday.

Late on Friday night the German Government, or rather the new German triumvirate—Hindenburg, Ludendorff, and Gröner—decided to muzzle the Reichstag for the whole winter to prevent public discussion of the extreme measures now to be taken.

The announcement made to the

From SIR DOUGLAS HA

France, S

TO W

TA

The fo
certified
net sale
proachin
lished b
should s
Truth P
own com
nnwise

WHY GERMANY WANTED WAR

MAY

BETHMANN'S FURY.

"ENGLAND'S MONSTROUS AIMS."

The following statement by the German Chancellor is nothing but the old and hopeless German trick of attempting to divide the Allies.

FROM OUR OWN CORRESPONDENT.

NEW YORK, Sunday.

The *New York World* to-day publishes a nebulous statement, sanctioned by Herr Bethmann Hollweg, the German Chancellor, and edited by Herr Zimmermann, the Foreign Under-Secretary, purporting to give the "objectives" of Germany. Primarily the statement is a tirade against Great Britain. All the Allies, it says, are fighting for conquest, but "the mo monstrous of all are England's aim

GREEK KING AGAIN.

STILL PLAYING WITH THE ALLIES.

From J. M. N. JEFFRIES.

ATHENS, Saturday Night.

Greece is confronted by another crisis to-day with the presentation of Admiral du Fournet's Note demanding the cession of destroyers, torpedo craft, and other light vessels of the Greek Fleet for service as coast guards and for protection against German submarines.

The Government, after a long Cabinet Council, over which the King presided, refused.

TEN MO
IN GERM

THE WOMAN

ALL HEI

VAGARIES OF TI FEMINI

CHAPTER
By D. THOMA

·CE.

he only al daily ven ap- ies pub- wspaper, ide-the- in their they are Public

Below: **The desolation of the Ancre Valley can be seen from these panoramic views taken from Hamel, looking toward Miramount.**

Bottom and opposite bottom: **Two maps suggesting why Germany is now keen for peace. The first shows the territory Germany occupied in 1914, the second illustrates the extent of the German Empire at the end of 1916.**

WHY GERMANY WANTS PEACE

October 1916

October 9, 1916 – The British continued to gain ground east of Le Sars.

In Britain, as the shortage of food supplies cut deep, a Royal Commission on Wheat supplies was established for the purchase, sale and control of wheat and flour.

October 10, 1916 – South of the Somme, French troops captured the village of Ablaincourt and the nearby Bois de Chaulnes.

A combined force of Austro-Hungarian and German troops invaded Romania and moved towards Bucharest.

October 12, 1916 – The British continued to advance on a four-mile front between the village of Eaucourt and the Bapaume-Péronne road.

October 13, 1916 – A Franco-British operation, consisting of 40 planes, dropped bombs on the Mauser rifle factory at Oberndorf in southern Germany.

October 14, 1916 – Although German troops were driven out of the southern side of the Schwaben Redoubt by the British after three days of fighting, they continued to hold the remainder of the strongpoint.

October 16, 1916 – French troops gained a foothold in the village of Sailly, two miles east of Morval.

October 17, 1916 – More French gains were made in Sailly-Saillisel.

After discussions with army commanders, Haig limited the scope of operations on the Somme in co-operation with the French Sixth Army.

October 18, 1916 – Further Allied attacks were mounted against the Germans at Gueudecourt and the British managed to make some gains to the north of the village. French troops captured Sailly-Saillisel to the south.

The relentless wet weather and atrocious conditions on the ground made progress slow and brought to an end the Battle of Le Transloy.

BEAUMONT-HAMEL STATION AS IT IS TO-DAY

"ALL CHANGE!"—THE RUINS OF BEAUMONT-HAMEL RAILWAY STATION AFTER OUR BOMBARDMENT.—This is the sight presented by the railway station of Beaumont-Hamel after its recent brilliant capture by our troops. The name of the station is still partly legible on the wall to the right. The railway lines are almost lost in the waste of debris caused by our shell-fire, and beyond the station is a grove of decapitated tree trunks. The whole is an all-sufficient comment on the German boast that we should "never take Beaumont-Hamel." [Official Photograph.

Above: **Most of Beaumont Hamel, including the railway station, was destroyed.**

Left: **A memorial to the German soldiers who fell when Beaumont Hamel was captured by the Allies.**

MORE GERMAN FORTS STORMED.

BRITISH CAPTURE BEAUCOURT

BEAUMONT CAVES "AS BIG AS BUCKINGHAM PALACE."

ADVANCE SOUTH OF BAPAUME

From GENERAL SIR DOUGLAS HAIG.

FRANCE, Tuesday, 10.50 a.m.

We have stormed the heavily fortified village of Beaumont-Hamel [west of the Ancre and north-west of Thiepval]. and have advanced to the outskirts of Beaucourt-sur-Ancre [a mile and a quarter east of Beaumont-Hamel].

The number of prisoners is increasing, and considerably over 4,000 have passed through the collecting stations since yesterday morning.

Fighting continues.

9.40 p.m.

The village of Beaucourt-sur-Ancre is in our hands.

Prisoners reported up to date number considerably over 5,000 and more are coming in.

To-day a successful local advance was made east of the Butte de Warlencourt (i.e., south of Bapaume). Practically all our objectives were gained and some 80 prisoners were taken in this area.

See the very large map in the Back Page.

TER BEAUMONT-HAMEL WAS STORMED—OFFICIAL PHOTOGRAPHS.

BRINGS IN HIS BOCHE.—Cowed, battered, and muddy, this strapping Beaumont-Hamel Hun is typical of hundreds of the prisoners we captured during the storming of the village. "Tommy" is seen escorting his prize along a railway track.

"D MEN—AND MORE MEN. WE CAN WIN ONLY BY KEEPING
ENEMY DAZED AND DESPAIRING."—Mr. Beach Thomas.

CAPTIVES FROM THE UNDER-WORLD OF BEAUMONT-HAMEL.—These German prisoners, formed up in one of the advance cages, are those who hid in the immense "dug-outs" under Beaumont-Hamel and in the dim caves which date from some far-off period, possibly "from the days of the Inquisition." From one cavern 400 enemy soldiers filed out meekly, says Mr. W. Beach Thomas, after the British attack was over. [Official Photograph.

CONGRATULATED BY THE KING.—
Douglas Haig, who has received the congrat
of the King on his success in the Ancre

Below: The site of Beaumont Hamel's church is reduced to rubble. The 51st Highland Division took the village on 13 November 1916, one of the Allies' final successes before Haig closed down the Somme offensive.

Right: Troops climb aboard the remains of a railway wagon destroyed by shellfire at Beaucourt.

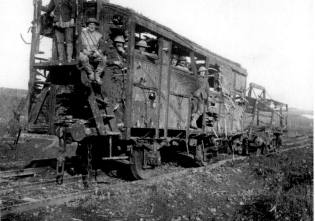

October 1916

October 19, 1916 – Cardinal Mercier of Belgium protested to the Germans against the deportation to Germany of Belgian workers.

October 20, 1916 – Heavy German attacks on Schwaben and Stuff Redoubts were fought off.

October 21, 1916 – British troops advanced further along a line of almost five kilometres between Schwaben and Le Sars.
Canadian troops captured parts of Regina Trench close to Thiepval.

October 23, 1916 – The Canadians tried to extend their control of Regina Trench but were held back by the mud and heavy German fire.
Sergeant Robert Downie was awarded the VC for charging and securing an enemy position near Lesbœufs.

October 25, 1916 – Allied forces carried out a bombing raid on the Thyssen steel works at Hagendingen north of Metz.

October 28, 1916 – German flying ace and commander of the Jasta 2 fighter squadron, Captain Oswald Boelcke, died in a mid-air collision with a fellow airman during a dogfight with planes of the Royal Flying Corps over Pozières.

October 30, 1916 – Hermann von Stein succeeded Adolf Wild von Hohenborn as German Minister of War. French troops moved north, taking trenches to the north-west of the already-captured French village of Sailly-Saillisel.

October 31, 1916 – British casualties for the previous three months were reported as more than 350,000 – approximately 40 per cent of total war casualties to date.

Opposite below: **Tommies on their way to the trenches pass through St Pol. They smile broadly at the camera knowing the photograph will be sent back to England.**

Opposite above: **Troops negotiate frozen ponds of muddy water in December 1916.**

Above: **The weather caused military operations to be temporarily suspended and men concentrated on survival in the freezing, wet conditions.**

HAIG'S NEW FEAT IN THE MUD.

GRANDCOURT.

**DING MIRAUMONT
MED.**

MILES FRONT.

**ED BACK BOTH
THE ANCRE.**

**BAD NEWS FROM
RUMANIA.**

PLAIN INVADED.

**IMPORTANT RAILWAY
REACHED.**

Bad news comes from Rumania. The Germans report that they have reached the railway which runs to Craiova and the Danube at a point apparently about 40 miles north-west of Craiova and considerably behind the Rumanian flank at the exit of the Vulcan Pass.

From CHARLES TOWER.

**RECAPTURE OF
MONASTIR.**

ENTRY OF SERBS.

HEAVY BLOW TO SOFIA

From J. M. N. JEFFRIES.
ATHENS, Sunday, 12.50 p.m.
Monastir was captured by the Serbians and the French last evening.

FRENCH OFFICIAL

ARM ALL SHIPS.

**HOW TO MEET U-BOAT
MENACE.**

MORE VESSELS SUNK.

The demand of *The Daily Mail* for the arming of all British merchantmen has brought expressions of approval from many quarters. Naval men and officers and men of the mercantile marine are especially vigorous in their support of the proposal.

"THE TI

**TO-DAY'S
IN P**

The Times is publ
first time since its
ago, at 1½d. a copy.
In the past the pri
changed, the highest
100 years ago, and t
tween March 16, 191
week. When the so-
ledge"—i.e., on new

107

The Somme: one million casualties

The village of Thiepval, taken on 25 September, had been a day-one objective. Other scraps of territory changed hands more than once, and always at a heavy human cost. Germany's determination to retake every inch of high ground conceded meant their losses, too, mounted. Haig was not about to blink, pressing on resolutely until the taking of Beaumont Hamel during the battle's final action allowed him to wind down the operation on a positive note. There should have been little cause for back-slapping as this had been another 1 July target.

As winter set in and stock was taken, it was self-evident that the blunt instrument of attrition rather than the rapier of penetration best characterised the 141 days of attack and counter. Having both objectives hovering over the battlefield was a boon to Haig, for although his grand design had not materialised, he could lay claim to seriously weakening the enemy's manpower, matériel and morale.

A century on, the cost-benefit analysis of the Somme campaign continues unabated. Seven miles was the maximum extent of the Allies' territorial gain. Early in the new year the German Army would willingly concede ground as they withdrew to the Hindenburg Line, shortening the front and conserving vital resources. And so the battle would be reckoned not in terms of a sweeping territorial success but how much damage had been inflicted upon the enemy. There were over a million casualties in total, shared in roughly equal measure. The grim statistics would forever taint Haig's reputation in the eyes of many, the Somme regularly invoked as an exemplar of crass leadership and prodigal futility. Apologists point to the mighty blow that was dealt the Kaiser's army, and that the Allies were left firmly on the front foot at the dawn of the new year. As one officer of the Reich put it, the Somme was "the muddy grave of the German field army".

WHAT THE SOMME FRONT LOOKS LIKE NOW.—This photograph gives a vivid idea of the meaning of the words "Somme Front." Mud, water, desolation and the nakedness of shell-swept woods tell how Northern France is being reduced to a wilderness. A long file of our men is seen coming along a muddy track which is being converted into a military road. [*Official Photograph.*]

The Somme was "the muddy grave of the German field army".

Above: A build-up of traffic on the muddy roads around the Somme. The graves of German soldiers can be seen on the right.

Left: Stretcher-bearers transport a Canadian infantryman to safety. Many conscientious objectors volunteered for this dangerous non-combat job where the casualty rate was high.

Douchy
St Amand
Hannescamps
Courcelles
les Essarts
Ablainzevelle
Courcellette
Thiepval
Mesnil
Baizieu
Bresle
Ville
Treux
Morlancourt
Suzanne
Mericourt
Bray

Above: The battle ground north of the Somme showing successive stages of the British advance from 1 July, as recounted from General Haig's despatch. The broken line at the top and right indicates the front at the end of 1916.

Opposite above: British troops trudge along the wet road that skirts swamps, shattered trees and broken buildings and vehicles. The cost of the Somme offensive was nearly 624,000 Allied casualties and a further 146,000 killed or missing.

Opposite below: Australian troops make their way to the trenches in December 1916.

November 1916

November 1, 1916 – At Sailly-Saillisel, north of the Somme, a German counter-attack was repulsed, whilst further north Allied troops advanced beyond Lesbœufs.

November 2, 1916 – Troops of the British Army captured enemy trenches east of Gueudecourt in the northern Somme.

November 5, 1916 – Although the Battle of Le Transloy officially ended on 18 October, a final unsuccessful attack was launched. The battle ended with no significant gain along the Transloy Ridge. Germany and Austria declared Poland an "independent state".
Lieutenant Eugene Bennett won his VC for his bravery when leading his men in an attack in the final days of the Somme Offensive at the Battle of Le Transloy.

November 6, 1916 – French troops made progress near St. Pierre Vaast Wood, south of Lesbœufs.

November 7, 1916 – East of the Butte de Warlencourt, British troops advanced further along the Albert-Bapaume road.
North of the Ancre, a German attack was repulsed west of Beaumont-Hamel.
The 1916 US Presidential election was held but the result was so close that the outcome remained in doubt for several days. In the end, Woodrow Wilson was re-elected.
Cardinal Mercier pleaded for further pressure to stop the German deportations of Belgian forced labour.

November 8, 1916 –The German submarine *U-49* sank the American steamer *Columbian* near Cape Finisterre on the Atlantic coast of Spain.

November 9, 1916 – An aerial battle took place between British and German planes above Bapaume on the Somme.

This page: **The defence** line was now stiffened by German troops. More than two million German men would meet their deaths before the war was over.

Opposite below: **Seven** miles was the maximum extent of the Allies' territorial gain during the Somme campaign.

Opposite above: **A** borrowed stove provides warmth and a much-needed cup of tea.

Above: "The Fighting Fifth" still cheering. The Northumberland Fusiliers celebrate the end of the Somme campaign.

November 1916

November 10, 1916 – British troops occupied the eastern section of the Regina Trench to the north of Thiepval.
Several German trenches to the northeast of Lesbœufs were captured by French troops.

November 11, 1916 – The Battle of the Ancre Heights ended with a British victory over German forces.
French troops completed their capture of Saillisel.

November 13, 1916 – In the final significant phase of the Somme offensive, the Battle of the Ancre began and saw a renewal of the Allied offensive; British troops finally captured Beaumont-Hamel and Beaucourt at the northern end of the Somme Front. Lieutenant Bernard Freyberg's courage and exemplary leadership earned him the VC in the final week of the offensive during an attack on Beaumont-Hamel.
Private John Cunningham won his VC on the opening day of the Battle of the Ancre, when he went forward with a bombing party.

November 15, 1916 – An inter-Allied conference was held in Paris to discuss ways to counter German mobilisation of Belgians and Poles. In an effort to regulate food consumption, the British Government appointed a Food Controller.

November 16, 1916 – The British line was extended eastwards from Beaucourt.

November 17, 1916 – The French airman, Captain de Beauchamp, flew on a daring raid to Munich, after which he crossed the Alps and landed near Venice.

November 18, 1916 – After four-and-half months of fighting, the Battle of the Somme ended with enormous losses on both sides. Allied forces had pushed back the German line by only a few miles and the major breakthrough the Allies had planned never occurred. The total cost to both sides exceeded one million casualties.

November 20, 1916 – The German diplomat Gottlieb von Jagow resigned as German Foreign Minister.

November 21, 1916 – Emperor Franz Josef I of Austria died and was succeeded by his great-nephew Charles I.

Casualties of war

The Royal Army Medical Corps numbered around 140,000 officers and men at its peak in World War One, by which time the triage system was in operation. The wounded were assessed and, if the injuries were superficial, treated on the spot at forward Aid Posts or Dressing Stations with a view to enabling the patient to return to duty quickly. Those with more serious wounds might be removed by field ambulance to a Casualty Clearing Station, and thence to a Base Hospital well behind the line if that was deemed appropriate. Repatriation was an option, and some soldiers struggling with the rigours of frontline service positively hankered after a "Blighty touch" – an injury that might see them shipped home to convalesce.

Torrential rains in October turned the battlegrounds on the Somme into a muddy quagmire and in mid-November the battle ended, with the Allies having advanced only 8 kilometres (five miles). The British suffered around 420,000 casualties, the French 195,000 and the Germans around 650,000.

Those who lay stricken on the battlefield owed much to the stretcher-bearers, who themselves risked life and limb in trying to render assistance. Transport to the Casualty Clearing Station might be by horse-drawn wagon or motorised vehicle; in either case travelling across uneven ground must have added greatly to the discomfort they were already experiencing. Those who could reach a treatment centre unaided did so – the "walking wounded". Casualty Clearing Stations were often located where there was easy access to the railway network, and many were invalided home minus a limb, for amputations were carried out at these treatment centres. Grim practicality meant cemeteries are often to be found where the stations were sited.

Initial assessments inevitably saw some placed in a third category: those whose wounds were so severe that the use of scarce resources could not be justified. The priority was to give attention not to those in greatest need but to those who would most benefit. Difficult decisions about likely outcomes had to be made, often in pressure-cooker circumstances.

Some hankered after a "Blighty touch" – an injury that might see them shipped home to convalesce.

Left: Once the wounded were brought clear of the battlefield, medical staff could begin triage and arrange medical care according to the severity of their injuries.

Below left: A wounded man is lifted from an ambulance wagon at a farmhouse hospital station. Over half of the injuries during the conflict were caused by shells or trench mortars but as the war progressed the number of gas casualties significantly increased.

Opposite below: Refreshments are provided for the walking wounded. During the conflict the British Red Cross and the Order of St John supported the Royal Army Medical Corps, forming a Joint War Committee.

Below: Red Cross ambulances on hand to support the medical services. At the beginning of the war there were around 9,000 medical staff mobilised from the Royal Army Medical Corps but by the time peace was declared they numbered almost 133,000. Nearly 7,000 medical staff were killed during the course of the war.

November 1916

November 24, 1916 – Boris Stürmer, a protégé of Rasputin, resigned as Russian Premier and Foreign Minister and was succeeded by Alexander Trepov as Premier.

November 26, 1916 – A German naval raid took place on Lowestoft, on the east coast of England, during which the naval trawler HMT *Narval* was sunk.

November 27, 1916 – Two Zeppelins were shot down during a German airship raid on Hartlepool and Great Yarmouth on England's east coast.

November 28, 1916 – The first German daylight air raid on London took place. The Germans hoped that by making the raids on London and the south-east, the British Air Force would be forced into protecting the home front rather than attacking the German Air Force.

November 29, 1916 – The British Government announced that vacant agricultural land would be taken under its control in an effort to boost food production.

December 1916

December 1, 1916 – Lloyd George declared his inability to remain in the Government.

December 5, 1916 – Prime Minister Herbert Asquith resigned.

December 7, 1916 – David Lloyd George replaced Asquith as Prime Minister.

December 9, 1916 – The new British War Cabinet was formed replacing the War Committee which had held its last meeting earlier in the month.

December 12, 1916 – Germany sued for peace, but the wording was such that Lloyd George rejected it as a "sham proposal".

December 18, 1916 – The longest battle on the Western Front, the Battle of Verdun, ended with huge losses but no tactical or strategical advantage gained by either side.
US President Woodrow Wilson issued a circular note asking all belligerents to state their war objectives, as a first step towards peace.

December 19, 1916 – The British Government instituted National Service.

December 25, 1916 – King George sent a message to the troops on the third Christmas Day of the Great War.

December 26, 1916 – An Anglo-French conference met in London to discuss the German and US Peace Notes.

December 30, 1916 – Rasputin, the confidante and confessor of the Russian Tsar's wife, Empress Alexandra, was murdered by two relatives of Tsar Nicholas II. Rasputin's influence over the Tsarina had increased greatly after using hypnotism to stop the bleeding of the haemophiliac heir to the throne, the Tsarevich Alexei Nikolaevich.
The Bulgarian Government accepted President Wilson's proposals for peace negotiations, but the Allied governments rejected the proposals put forward by German Chancellor Hollweg.

This page: **A century on, the cost-benefit analysis of the Somme campaign continues unabated. Seven miles was the maximum extent of the Allies' territorial gain.**

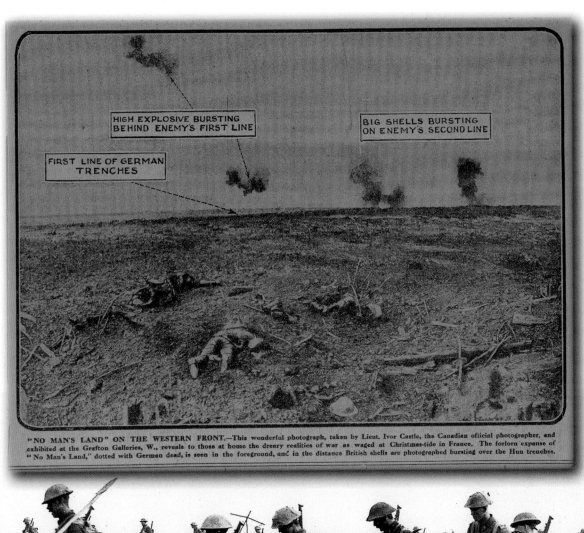

HIGH EXPLOSIVE BURSTING
BEHIND ENEMY'S FIRST LINE

BIG SHELLS BURSTING
ON ENEMY'S SECOND LINE

FIRST LINE OF GERMAN
TRENCHES

"NO MAN'S LAND" ON THE WESTERN FRONT.—This wonderful photograph, taken by Lieut. Ivor Castle, the Canadian official photographer, and exhibited at the Grafton Galleries, W., reveals to those at home the dreary realities of war as waged at Christmas-tide in France. The forlorn expanse of "No Man's Land," dotted with German dead, is seen in the foreground, and in the distance British shells are photographed bursting over the Hun trenches.

Sir Douglas Haig

Among the most controversial figures in British military history, Douglas Haig still divides opinion a century on from the campaigns with which his name is most closely associated. Advocates highlight the single-mindedness and strength of purpose of a leader who played a significant role in turning the war in the Allies' favour in 1918. Critics point to reckless offensives that were shockingly wasteful of human life. Positions taken in assessing Haig's contribution tend to be as entrenched and immovable as the Western Front itself. Was he the heroic architect of a famous victory over the Central Powers? Or prime candidate for the asinine role in the oft-quoted assessment that British troops were "lions led by donkeys"?

Born in Edinburgh on 19 June 1861, Haig was a career soldier from the moment he left Oxford and entered Sandhurst. In his climb through the ranks he served with the 7th Hussars before studying at the Staff College at Camberley, where he was a contemporary of another distinguished World War One leader, Sir Edmund Allenby. Haig saw action in Sudan in the Boer conflict before being posted to India, where he was appointed Inspector-General of Cavalry. By 1906 he was back at the War Office, where his duties included drafting training manuals. He also played a key role in establishing the Territorial Army, replacing a reservist system that was in need of overhaul. He was made General Officer Commanding at Aldershot, spiritual home of the British Army, and from there he prepared Ist Corps for action as part of the British Expeditionary Force, which mobilised when war was declared on 4 August.

Haig was promoted to full general after the first Battle of Ypres ended in November 1914, and a month later was chosen to command the newly formed 1st Army. In December 1915 Haig replaced Sir John French as Commander-in-Chief of the BEF, and in an effort to break the stalemate that had set in along the Western Front embarked on a series of offensives that incurred a high casualty toll. The former cavalry officer had to adapt to new-style trench warfare. Some said the fact that he persisted with frontal assaults at the Somme and Passchendaele showed that he did not adapt quickly enough; and that he was slow to recognise the importance of new technology. Long after the guns of World War One fell silent Haig was of the view that "aeroplanes and tanks are only accessories to a man on a horse". Others argue that his methods did ultimately wear down the enemy and pave the way to victory. Haig was righteous and uncompromising, his bulldog tenacity undoubtedly one of his great strengths. He maintained an unswerving belief in the application of pressure as the key to achieving a breakthrough. As losses mounted and some – Lloyd George among them – questioned the wisdom of such a strategy, Haig's clarion call was for a redoubling of effort. To apply the brake

and allow the enemy time to recover was the real folly. That unyielding attitude led him to state that casualties totalling 120,000 in the first month of the Somme offensive "cannot be regarded as sufficient to justify any anxiety as to our ability to continue the offensive". With such comments admirable tenacity spilled over into reckless disregard from the critics' stance.

Germany's spring offensive of 1918 brought a response from Haig that showed his steely resolve. "There is no other course open to us but to fight it out. Every position must be held to the last man; there must be no retirement. With our backs to the wall, and believing in the justice of our cause, each one of us must fight to the end." Marshal Foch was made supreme commander of Allied forces as the war reached its critical point, but Haig's army was prominent in the battles that brought the conflict to an end.

The granting of a peerage, plus the sum of £100,000, was indicative of how the Establishment viewed Haig's achievements. He retired in 1921, devoting the last years of his life to improving the lot of ex-servicemen through the Royal British Legion, which he helped set up. Following his death on 28 January 1928, aged 66, a *Times* eulogy referred to the Somme campaign, pointing out that the heavy human cost was sometimes accorded undue prominence over the gains: namely, helping relieve Verdun and delivering a damaging blow to the German spirit. "In the judgment of history," it concluded, "it may be that the country will recognise the wisdom and discount the cost."

Over 80 years on, that judgment remains in the balance.

Left: (l to r) Albert Thomas, the French Minister of Munitions; Sir Douglas Haig; General Joffre and David Lloyd George at the 4th Army Headquarters at Méaulte on 12 September 1916.

Opposite below right: Haig was a very adept horseman and a talented polo player. He represented England on a tour of the USA and had become Chairman of the Hurlingham Polo Committee in 1914.

Haig maintained an unswerving belief in the application of pressure as the key to achieving a breakthrough.

SIR D. HAIG'S DESPATCH ON THE SOMME.
December 30, 1916

Sir Douglas Haig's despatch on the Somme battle – from July 1 to November 18 – is published below. It concludes with the following confident words: –

The enemy's power has not yet been broken, nor is it yet possible to form an estimate of the time the war may last before the objects for which the Allies are fighting have been attained. But the Somme battle has placed beyond doubt the ability of the Allies to gain those objects.

The German Army is the mainstay of the Central Powers, and a full half of that Army, despite all the advantages of the defensive, supported by the strongest fortifications, suffered defeat on the Somme this year.

Neither victors nor the vanquished will forget this; and, though bad weather has given the enemy a respite, there will undoubtedly be many thousands in his ranks who will begin the new campaign with little confidence in their ability to resist our assaults or to overcome our defence.

Our new Armies entered the battle with the determination to win and with confidence in their power to do so. They have proved to themselves, to the enemy, and to the world that this confidence was justified, and in the fierce struggle they have been through they have learned many valuable lessons which will help them in the future.

SIR DOUGLAS HAIG WRITES:

The three main objects with which we had commenced our offensive in July had already (by November 18) been achieved, in spite of the fact that the heavy autumn rains had prevented full advantage being taken of the favourable situation created by our advance, at a time when we have good grounds for hoping to achieve yet more important successes.

Verdun had been relieved; the main German forces had been held on the western front; and the enemy's strength had been very considerably worn down.

Any one of these three results is in itself sufficient to justify the Somme battle. The attainment of all three of them affords ample compensation for the splendid efforts of our troops and for the sacrifices made by ourselves and

our Allies. They have brought us a long step forward towards the final victory of the Allied cause.

The desperate struggle for the possession of Verdun had invested that place with a moral and political importance out of all proportion to its military value. Its fall would undoubtedly have been proclaimed as a great victory for our enemies, and would have shaken the faith of many in our ultimate success. The failure of the enemy to capture it, despite great efforts and very heavy losses, was a severe blow to his prestige, especially in view of the confidence he had openly expressed as to the results of the struggle.

GERMANS TIED TO THE WEST.

Information obtained both during the progress of the Somme battle and since the suspension of active operations has fully established the effect of our offensive in keeping the enemy's main forces tied to the western front. A movement of German troops eastward, which had commenced in June as a result of the Russian successes, continued for a short time only after the opening of the Allied attack. Thereafter the enemy forces that moved east consisted with one exception, of divisions that had been exhausted in the Somme battle, and these troops were always replaced on the western front by fresh divisions.

In November the strength of the enemy in the western theatre of war was greater than in July, notwithstanding the abandonment of his offensive at Verdun. It is possible that if Verdun had fallen large forces might still have been employed in an endeavour further to exploit that success. It is, however, far more probable, in view of developments in the eastern theatre, that a considerable transfer of troops in that direction would have followed. It is therefore justifiable to conclude that the Somme offensive not only relieved Verdun but held large forces which would otherwise have been employed against our Allies in the east.

The third great object of the Allied operations on the Somme was the wearing down of the enemy's powers of resistance. Any statement of the extent

to which this has been attained must depend in some degree on estimates. There is, nevertheless, sufficient evidence to place it beyond doubt that the enemy's losses in men and material have been very considerably higher than those of the Allies, while morally the balance of advantage on our side is still greater.

FEEBLE RESISTANCE.

During the period under review a steady deterioration took place in the morale of large numbers of the enemy's troops. Many of them, it is true, fought with the greatest determination, even in the latest encounters, but the resistance of still larger numbers became latterly decidedly feebler than it had been in the earlier stages of the battle. Aided by the great depth of his defences and by the frequent reliefs which his resources in men enabled him to effect, discipline and training held the machine together sufficiently to enable the enemy to rally and reorganise his troops after each fresh defeat.

As our advance progressed, four-fifths of the total number of divisions engaged on the western front were thrown one after another into the Somme battle, some of them twice and some three times; and towards the end of the operations when the weather unfortunately broke there can be no doubt that his power of resistance had been very seriously diminished.

ACCOMPLISHMENTS SO FAR

The total number of prisoners taken by us in the Somme battle between July 1 and November 18 is just over 38,000, including over 800 officers. During the same period we captured 29 heavy guns, 96 field guns and field howitzers, 136 trench mortars, and 514 machine-guns.

So far as these results are due to the action of the British forces, they have been attained by troops the vast majority of whom had been trained during the war. Many of them, especially among the drafts sent to replace wastage, counted their service by months, and gained in the Somme battle their first experience of war. The conditions under which we entered the war had made this

FASHIONING THE NEW ENGLAND

By LORD NORTHCLIFFE.

Owing to the great demand for " The Weekly Dispatch " yesterday, many of our readers were unable to get Lord Northcliffe's article on the situation, and on their request we reprint it below. The article was a telegram which was sent to nearly one thousand United States, Canadian, Australasian, French, Italian, South American, and other journals.

We have been making history in London during this last week. We are fashioning a new England, an England that is well worth watching.

The silver lining to the cloud of war is the fact that more social reforms have been accomplished in Great Britain in the two years and a half of struggle than in the previous hundred years of peace.

The burden of taxation has been increased on the shoulders best able to bear it—the very rich. Our railways have come under Government control. The sale of alcohol is becoming more and more regulated. The youth of the nation is being trained in healthy military exercise with effects observable by everyone. Labour is taking its proper place in Government councils. Workers are being better remunerated. I could name a

THE PREMIER. [*Photograph by Vandyk.*]

Above: David Lloyd George acknowledges the cheers from British troops as he emerges from a captured German dug-out at Fricourt.

unavoidable. We were compelled either to use hastily trained and inexperienced officers and men, or else to defer the offensive until we had trained them. In this latter case we should have failed our Allies.

That these troops should have accomplished so much under such conditions, and against an army and a nation whose chief concern for so many years has been preparation for war, constitutes a feat of which the history of our nation records no equal. The difficulties and hardships cheerfully overcome, and the endurance, determination, and invincible courage shown in meeting them, can hardly be imagined by those who have not had personal experience of the battle, even though they have themselves seen something of war.

THE STORMED FORTRESSES.

Dealing with the various branches of the Army Sir Douglas says:

Against such defences as we had to assault – far more formidable in many respects than those of the most famous fortresses in history – infantry would have been powerless without thoroughly efficient artillery preparation and support. The work of our artillery was wholly admirable, though the strain on the personnel was enormous. The excellence of the results attained was the more remarkable in view of the shortness of the training of most of the junior officers and of the N.C.O.s and men. Despite this, they rose to a very high level of technical and tactical skill, and the combination between artillery and infantry, on which, above everything, victory depends, was an outstanding feature of the battle. Good even in July, it improved with experience, until in the later assaults it approached perfection.

In this combination between infantry and artillery the Royal Flying Corps played a highly important part. The admirable work of this corps has been a very satisfactory feature of the battle.

The greatest skill and daring have been shown in the performance of all these duties, as well as in bombing expeditions. Our Air Service has also co-operated with our infantry in their assaults, signalling the position of our attacking troops and turning machine-guns on to the enemy infantry and even on to his batteries in action.

NEED OF NEWEST AEROPLANES.

Not only had the work of the Royal Flying Corps to be carried out in all weathers and under constant fire from the ground, but fighting in the air has now become a normal procedure in order to maintain the mastery over the enemy's air service. In these fights the greatest skill and determination have been shown, and great success has attended the efforts of the Royal Flying Corps.

I desire to point out, however, that the maintenance of mastery in the air, which is essential, entails a constant and liberal supply of the most up-to-date machines, without which even the most skilful pilots cannot succeed.

PROFICIENCY OF PERSONNEL.

Trench mortars, both heavy and light, have become important, and valuable work has been done by the personnel. They are likely to be employed even more frequently in future.

Machine-guns play a great part – almost a decisive part under some conditions – in modern war, and our Machine Gun Corps has attained to considerable proficiency in their use, handling them with great boldness and skill. The highest value of these weapons is displayed on the defensive rather than in the offensive, and we were attacking. Nevertheless, in attack also machine-guns can exercise very great influence in the hands of men with a quick eye for opportunity and capable of a bold initiative. The Machine Gun Corps, though comparatively recently formed, has done very valuable work and will increase in importance.

The part played by the "tanks" has been brought to notice by me in my daily reports. These cars proved of great value on various occasions, and the personnel in charge of them performed many deeds of remarkable valour.

As to gas and liquid flame, the Army owes its thanks to the chemists, physiologists, and physicists of the highest rank who devoted their energies to enabling us to surpass the enemy in the use of a means of warfare which took the civilised world by surprise. Our own experience of the numerous experiments and trials necessary before gas and flame could be used, of the great preparations for their manufacture, and of the special training required for the personnel,

shows that the employment of such methods by the Germans was not the result of a desperate decision, but had been prepared for deliberately. The enemy has suffered heavy casualties from our gas attacks, while the means of protection adopted by us have proved thoroughly effective.

After recording the services of other branches of the Army and "the obligations of the Army to the Navy for the unfailing success" of transport of men and material, Sir Douglas says:

WORKERS AT HOME.

I also desire to record the obligation of the Army in the Field to the various authorities at home, and to the workers under them – women as well as men – by whose efforts and self-sacrifice all our requirements were met. Without the vast quantities of munitions and stores of all sorts provided, and without the drafts of men sent to replace wastage, the efforts of our troops could not have been maintained.

He pays tribute to the medical services – "the immense help of the British Red Cross" is specially mentioned – and praises Generals Sir Henry Rawlinson and Sir Hubert, the Staff work, and the splendid French Army.

Opposite top right: Soldiers home on Christmas leave buy their turkeys at a stall near Victoria Station.

Opposite top left: British troops negotiate with a French market trader for some mistletoe for their billet.

Opposite middle: Christmas dinner for these men is bread, jam and tea in a shell hole at Beaumont Hamel, next to the graveside of one of their comrades.

Opposite bottom: A cheery group, complete with a pet dog, are home on leave from France.

Soldiers from a battalion of the Durham Light Infantry raise their steel helmets on their rifles. Most of these men came from Sunderland.

Published by Atlantic Publishing in 2016
Atlantic Publishing
38 Copthorne Road, Croxley Green
Hertfordshire, WD3 4AQ, UK

ISBN Hardback: 978-1-909242 -84-5
ISBN Paperback: 978-1-909242-81-4

Printed in China

Acknowledgements:
Newspaper photography: Harry Chambers
Contemporary map: Malcolm Swanston

Thanks to:
The team at Associated Newspapers without whose help this book would not have been possible.
Particular thanks to: Rachel Swanston, Jonathan Baines and Alan Pinnock.

Thanks also to: Sarah Rickayzen, John Dunne and Cliff Salter